A VISITOR FROM OUTER SPACE

SCIENCE-FICTION STORIES
BY SOVIET WRITERS

Fredonia Books
Amsterdam. The Netherlands

A visitor from Outer Space:
Science-Fiction Stories by Soviet Writers

By
Alexander Belayev, Alexander Kazantsev
Vladimir Savchenko, Gerogy Gurevich
Arkady Strugatsky and Boris Strugatski

ISBN: 1-58963-331-8

Reprinted from the original edition

Fredonia Books
Amsterdam, The Netherlands
http://www.fredoniabooks.com

In order to make original editions of historical works available to scholars at an economical price, this facsimile of the original edition is reproduced from the best available copy and has been digitally enhanced to improve legibility, but the text remains unaltered to retain historical authenticity.

CONTENTS

A. BELAYEV

HOITY-TOITY

Professor Wagner's Invention
Material for His Biography Collected by A. Belayev

I. An Extraordinary Artiste

The huge Busch circus in Berlin was packed to capacity.
Silent as bats the waiters flitted about the steep balconies with
mugs of beer. Where the lids of beer-mugs stood open, indicating unslaked thirsts, they replaced them with full mugs
planted straight on the floor. Then off they hurried in response to the beckoning of more thirsty people. Stout mammas
with their still unmarried daughters unfolded grease-proof pa-
per packets; they munched sandwiches and ate black pud-
ding and Frankfurter sausages in profound concentration, their
eyes fixed on the arena.

However, it should be said for the spectators that neither
the fakir who tortured himself nor the man who swallowed
frogs was what attracted them in such vast numbers. They
were all waiting impatiently for the first part to end, the
entr'acte to be over, for then Hoity-Toity would do his turns.
Marvellous stories were told of him; people wrote articles
about him; scientists showed interest in him. He was an enigma, a general favourite and—a magnet. Ever since his first
appearance the "All tickets sold" notice had hung daily on
the circus box office. He could attract the sort of people who

had never set foot in the circus before. True, both gallery and pit were filled with regular circus-goers: small officials and workers with their families, shopkeepers, counter-hands. But elderly, grey-haired, serious-minded, even gloomy-looking people in somewhat old-fashioned overcoats and raincoats occupied the boxes and stalls. And in the front stalls there were also a few young people who were equally serious and taciturn. These people neither munched sandwiches nor drank beer. They sat very still, withdrawn into themselves like Brahmin priests. They were waiting for the second part of the performance, for Hoity-Toity, whom they had specially come to see.

During the entr'acte the only conversation had been about Hoity-Toity's coming performance. And now the learned men in the front stalls began to show signs of life. The long-awaited moment at last arrived. There was a flourish of trumpets, the circus attendants in their red and gold liveries lined up, the entrance curtains were drawn wide apart and, to a round of applause from the audience, Hoity-Toity came forward—a huge elephant, a cap embroidered in gold thread with strings and tassels on his head. With his attendant, a little man in a frock-coat, who bowed to the left and to the right, the elephant circled the arena. Then he moved to the centre and stood still, waiting.

"African," whispered a grey-haired professor to his colleague.

"I much prefer Indian elephants. Their bodies are more rounded. They give the impression of being more cultured, if one may use such an expression. The African elephant is clumsier-looking, more angular. When that sort of elephant stretches out its trunk, it looks like some sort of bird of prey."

The little man in the frock-coat standing by the elephant cleared his throat.

"Ladies and gentlemen!" he began. "Here I have' the honour to present to you our famous elephant, Hoity-Toity. His body is fourteen and a half feet long, his height is eleven and a half feet. From the tip of the trunk to the tip of the tail is nine metres."

Hoity-Toity suddenly raised his trunk and flourished it in front of the attendant.

"Ah, excuse me, I'm wrong," he said. "The trunk is two metres long and the tail about one and a half metres. Thus, the length from the tip of the trunk to the end of the tail is seven and nine-tenths metres. His daily consumption is three hundred and sixty-five kilograms of vegetables and sixteen buckets of water daily."

"The elephant's calculations appear to be better than the man's!" a voice was heard to say.

"Did you notice how the elephant corrected his trainer when he made a mistake?" asked the zoology professor of his colleague.

"Pure accident," retorted the other.

"Hoity-Toity is the most remarkable elephant in the world," continued the trainer, "and probably the greatest genius of all times among animals. He understands German. You do, don't you, Hoity?" he added, addressing the elephant.

Solemnly the elephant nodded. There was a burst of applause from the audience.

"Jiggery-pokery!" said Professor Schmidt.

"Ah, but you just see what comes next," objected Stolz. "Hoity-Toity can count and distinguish figures."

"Enough of the explanations! Show us!" shouted a voice from the gallery.

"To avoid any misunderstanding," continued the trainer, unruffled, "I would ask a few spectators to come down into

7

the arena, so that they can assure you that there is no trickery."

Schmidt and Stolz exchanged glances, then proceeded to the arena.

And then Hoity-Toity began to demonstrate his amazing gifts. Figures drawn on large squares of cardboard were placed in front of him, and he added, multiplied and divided by selecting from the heap of figures those which corresponded to the results of his calculations. One-figure numbers passed to two-figure, then to three-figure; the elephant solved every problem without a single mistake.

"Well? Now what have you to say?" asked Stolz.

"All right. We'll see how much he understands figures," replied Schmidt, grudgingly. With that he took his watch from his pocket, held it up and asked the elephant: "Would you mind telling us the time, Hoity-Toity?"

With a sudden movement of his trunk the elephant seized the watch from Schmidt's hand, dangled it before his eyes, returned it to its embarrassed owner and formed the reply using the cardboard squares:

"10.25."

Schmidt looked at the watch and shrugged in dismay; the elephant had told the time correct to the minute.

The next problem was reading. The trainer spread large pictures of animals in front of the elephant. Other cardboard sheets bore the inscriptions: lion, monkey, elephant. The elephant was first shown a picture of an animal, then with his trunk he indicated the cardboard sheet which bore the corresponding name. Not once did he make a mistake. Schmidt tried to alter the arrangement of the experiment: he showed the elephant the word and urged him to find the corresponding picture. The elephant did so again without a mistake.

Finally the whole alphabet was laid out in front of Hoity-

Toity. He now had to select letters, form words and reply to questions.

"What's your name?" asked Professor Stolz.

"Hoity-Toity ... now," replied the elephant.

"What do you mean ... 'now'?" asked Schmidt, joining in. "Had you another name before? What was it?"

"Sapiens,"* replied the elephant.

"Homo sapiens,** perhaps?" said Stolz with a chuckle.

"Perhaps," retorted the elephant, enigmatically.

He then proceeded to pick out letters to form the words: "And that's quite enough for today."

Ignoring the trainer's cries of protest, Hoity-Toity bowed in all directions and left the arena.

During the interval the professors assembled in the smoke-room; there they split up into groups and entered into lively conversation.

In a far corner Schmidt and Stolz were arguing together.

"Don't you remember, my dear fellow, the sensation Hans caused some time ago?" he was saying. "He was a horse and could give you the square root of a number and make all sorts of calculations, stamping out the replies with his hoof. And later it transpired that all it amounted to was that when his master gave him some hidden signal, he stamped his hoof in response. He could no more calculate than a blind puppy."

"That's just supposition," objected Stolz.

"Then what about the experiments of Thorndyke and Yorks? They were all based on the art of training the animals' natural associations. The animals were lined up in front of a series of boxes, only one of which contained food. Now say this particular box was the second from the right.

* Sapiens (Lat.)—wise.

** Homo Sapiens (Lat.)—wise man—the scientific name for man, in the classification of the mammals.

If the animal guesses which box contains food, it automatically opens and the animal gets food. Thus, a definite association, roughly speaking, develops in the animal: 'the second box from the right—food.' Then the boxes are arranged differently."

"You don't happen to have a food box in your watch," remarked Stolz, ironically. "Anyway, how do you explain the facts?"

"Why, the elephant didn't understand anything at all about my watch. He merely raised a shiny ring to his eyes. When he began selecting numbers on the cardboard squares, he was obviously only listening to some sort of instructions from the trainer which we could not perceive. It's all trickery, starting with the moment Hoity-Toity 'corrected' his trainer when he made a miscalculation of the elephant's length. Conditioned reflex—nothing more."

"I have the permission of the circus manager to stay behind with some of my colleagues after the performance. I'm going to try a few experiments on Hoity-Toity," said Stolz. "I take it you'll join us?"

"Most certainly," replied Schmidt.

II. The Personal Affront Was Just Too Much

When the circus was finally cleared of spectators and all the lights, save one over the arena, were extinguished, Hoity-Toity was again led in. Schmidt requested the trainer to absent himself during the experiments. The little man had removed his frock-coat and now wore a sweater. He shrugged and said nothing.

"Don't be offended ... er, forgive me, I don't know your name," began Schmidt.

"Jung, Friedrich Jung, at your service."

10

"Now see here, don't be offended, Herr Jung. We wish to arrange the experiment so that the whole affair will be above suspicion."

"Go ahead," replied the trainer. "Call me when you want the elephant led out." He marched off to the exit.

The scientists began their experiments. The elephant was attentive, obedient, answered questions and solved all sorts of problems without making a mistake. What he did was astounding. No training or trickery could explain his prompt replies. The extraordinary intelligence, almost human intellect, that the elephant possessed simply had to be admitted. Schmidt was half convinced by now, but he persisted in arguing out of stubbornness.

Meanwhile the elephant had evidently grown tired of listening to the endless arguing. Suddenly, with a deft movement of the trunk, he took Schmidt's watch from his waistcoat pocket and displayed it to its owner. The hands pointed to twelve. Then, after returning the watch, Hoity-Toity hoisted Schmidt by the scruff of the neck and carried him across the arena to the exit. The professor yelled in fury, but his colleagues did nothing but laugh. Jung rushed down the passage from the stables and began shouting at the elephant, but Hoity-Toity ignored him. Having · settled accounts with Schmidt by setting him down in the passage-way, he turned a baleful eye on the other scientists in the arena.

"It's all right, we're just going," said Stolz to the elephant just as though he were a human being. "Now, don't put yourself out!"

With that, Stolz left the arena covered with embarrassment and followed by the other professors.

"You were quite right, Hoity, to show them the door," said Jung. "We've a lot of work to do. Hi, Johann! Friedrich! Wilhelm! Where are you?"

Several workers appeared in the arena and began clearing up: they raked the sand, swept the passages, carried out the poles, ladders and hoops. The elephant, meanwhile, helped Jung to remove the decor. But somehow he seemed unwilling to work. He was annoyed about something or just tired, perhaps, after the second session at an unusual hour in the night. He snorted, tossed his head about and banged the decorations. He tugged so hard at one of them that it broke.

"Careful, you devil, you!" shouted Jung at him. "Why are you shirking the work? I suppose you fancy yourself. You can read and write, so manual work isn't to your liking! But there's nothing for it, old chap. This isn't an almshouse. Everybody works in the circus. Take Henrique Ferri. He's known all over the world as one of the best riders, yet when he's not doing his turn he's all dressed up in livery in the line-up, with the stablemen. And he'll take a turn at raking the sand."

It was true and the elephant knew it. But Hoity-Toity was not concerned with Henrique Ferri. He snorted again and set off to cross the arena to the passage.

"Hi, where are you off to?" yelled Jung, now thoroughly angry. "Stop! Stop, I tell you!"

He grabbed a broom, rushed at the elephant and struck his thick haunches with the handle. Jung had never struck the elephant before. True, the elephant had never before been so disobedient. Suddenly Hoity-Toity trumpeted so loudly that little Jung doubled up on the floor, his hands grasping his stomach, as though the sound made him feel sick. The elephant turned back, grabbed Jung like a puppy, tossed him up in the air several times and caught him each time in mid air. Finally he sat him down on the floor, picked up the broom and wrote in the sand, as he trundled about the arena:

"Don't you dare to strike me! I'm not an animal, I'm a human being!"

With that accomplished, he threw down the broom and shambled to the exit. He passed the horses in their stalls and reached the gate. There he leaned his enormous body against it and pressed hard with his shoulder. The gate creaked and then, giving way to the terrible pressure, splintered and fell into pieces. The elephant walked out to freedom.

———

Ludwig Strom was the circus manager, and as it happened he had spent a most disturbed night. When he was just dozing off at last, the butler tapped lightly on the bedroom door and announced that Jung had arrived on urgent business. Now the circus staff was well trained. Strom knew that something most serious must have happened for someone to be disturbing him at such an hour. He flung on his dressing-gown, slipped his feet into his slippers and went to the small sitting-room.

"What's wrong, Jung?" he asked.

"Something terrible, Herr Strom! Hoity-Toity's gone berserk!" Jung's eyes rolled and his arms waved about helplessly.

"Have you quite taken leave of your senses, Jung?" Strom inquired.

"I see, you don't believe me!" cried Jung, taking offence. "I'm quite sober, and in my full senses. If you don't believe me you can ask Johann, Friedrich and Wilhelm. They witnessed it all. The elephant wrenched the broom from my hands and wrote in the sand on the arena: 'I'm not an animal, I'm a human being!' Then he tossed me up to the big top sixteen times, walked off to the stables, smashed down the gate and escaped."

"What? Escaped! Why didn't you say so at once, you fool? We must set to work at once to catch him and fetch him back, otherwise he'll cause some mischief."

Strom could already see the chit from the police demand-ing a fine, the long bills for damage to fields from farmers, the summonses for the payment of large sums of money to cover the damage the elephant would cause.

"Who's on duty at the circus today? Have the police been informed? What's been done to catch the elephant?"

"It's my turn on duty. I've done everything I could," Jung replied. "I've not informed the police, they'll know soon enough. I chased after Hoity-Toity, I implored him to return. I addressed him as baron, count, even generalissimo. 'Come back, your Highness! Come back, your Grace! Forgive me for not recognizing you at once, but it was dark in the circus and I mistook you for an elephant,' I said. But he just threw a glance at me, trumpeted loudly with contempt and hurried on. Johann and Wilhelm are after him on motorbikes. He got out into the Unter den Linden, followed the Charlottenburger Chaussee through the length of the Tiergarten and made for Grünewald. At the moment he's wallowing in the Havel."

Just then the telephone rang and Strom picked up the receiver.

"Hallo! Yes, speaking.. I know already, thank you.... We've done what we could.... The fire brigade? I doubt it, better not irritate the animal."

"That was the police," said Strom, hanging up. "They suggest calling out the fire brigade, turning the hoses on the elephant to drive him back. But we need to go very carefully with Hoity-Toity."

"Madmen mustn't be aggravated," remarked Jung.

"All the same, Jung, the elephant knows you better than anyone else. Just try to get close to him and entice him gently back to the circus."

"I can try, of course. Perhaps I should address him as Hindenburg?"

Jung left. All night long Strom stayed up taking telephone messages and issuing instructions. For some time the elephant continued bathing just off Pfaueninsel island; then he raided an adjacent kitchen garden, ate up all the cabbages and carrots, tried the apples in a neighbouring orchard, and then made off for the Friedensdorf Woods.

None of the reports indicated that the elephant had done any harm to people or caused any wilful damage. In general he had behaved pretty well. He had carefully kept to the garden paths to avoid trampling the grass; he had tried to keep to the lanes and highways. Only hunger had compelled him to go for the vegetables and fruit in gardens and orchards. Even so, he had shown great care; he had not wilfully trampled on the beds, he had partaken methodically of the cabbages, consuming them row by row, and he had not torn down the branches of the fruit-trees.

At six in the morning Jung put in a second appearance; he was tired and dusty, his face was begrimed and sweaty, his clothing soaking wet.

"Well, how are things, Jung?"

"Nothing to report. Hoity-Toity refuses to respond to any form of persuasion. I even called him 'Herr President,' but he got wild and tossed me into the lake. Megalomania in elephants evidently takes a form that is different from what it is in people. So I tried to persuade him with rational arguments: 'Perhaps you imagine you're in Africa,' I asked him, afraid to use any title this time. 'This isn't Africa, it's latitude 52.5 N. Maybe it's August now and there's plenty of fruit and vegetables. But how about when the winter frost comes? What will you do then? You'll hardly eat bark, like the goats do, will you? Just you remember that once upon a time your ancestors, the mammoths, used to live here in Europe, but they all died out because of the cold. So hadn't you better go home to the circus, where you'll be housed, warmed and clothed?' Hoity-Toity listened most attentively, then he considered for a moment, but in the end he showered water on me from his trunk. Two baths in five minutes! I've had just about enough of it! It'll be a miracle if I've not caught a bad chill!"

III. A Declaration of War

All attempts at moral persuasion were of no avail. In the end Strom had to resort to decisive measures. A brigade of firemen was sent to the forest. Led by the police, the firemen approached to within ten yards of the elephant and formed a semi-circle; then they trained their strongest jets of water on the huge animal. The elephant thoroughly enjoyed the shower-bath, simply turning first one side, then the other to the hoses and snorting loudly. Then ten hoses were combined to make one strong jet of water and aimed the water straight at the elephant's eyes.

This he did not like. He trumpeted and advanced so resolutely upon the firemen that they wavered, then dropped their hoses and turned tail. In a trice the hoses were torn apart and fire-engines overturned.

From that moment the bills Strom was expected to pay mounted steadily. The elephant's anger was thoroughly aroused. War was declared between him and the people, and he did his best to indicate that the war was going to be costly for the people. He threw a number of the fire-brigade cars into the lake; he demolished the forester's lodge; he captured a policeman and tossed him up into a tree. He had previously acted with caution, but now there were no limits to the amount of harm he was causing. And yet, even in this work of destruction there were still the same signs of a peculiar sagacity; still he was quite capable of causing considerably more damage than the average elephant, even when maddened.

As soon as the Chief of Police received the report of the events in Friedensdorf Woods, he gave orders for large squads of police with rifles to be mobilized and dispatched to the forest to cordon it off and kill the elephant. Strom was in despair: he could never hope to find such an elephant again. He had already reconciled himself to the thought that he would have to pay dearly for the elephant's misdeeds. But Hoity-Toity, once he had returned to his senses, would pay him back in full and with interest. Strom implored the Chief of Police to postpone putting the order into force, in the hope that the obstreperous elephant could somehow be brought to heel.

"I can give you just ten hours," was the Chief of Police's reply. "In an hour's time the entire forest will be cordoned off. If necessary I shall call in the troops to assist the police."

Strom called an emergency meeting which was attended by almost all the staff and circus performers. The Director of the Zoological Gardens and his assistants were also present. Five hours after the meeting the forest was dotted with concealed pits and traps. Any ordinary elephant could easily be caught in such cunningly placed traps. But not Hoity-Toity! He stepped round the barriers, tore aside the camouflage over the pits, avoided setting a foot on the boards which were connected to heavy logs strung from the branches of the trees. If a log of that kind fell on the head of an elephant it would stun and fell the animal.

The time interval was coming to an end. Strong squads drew the cordon tighter and tighter. Armed police drew close to the lake where the elephant's huge body was already visible among the tree-trunks. He was busy filling his trunk with water, raising it over his head and letting the water fall in a fountain of spray like rain on his broad back.

"Ready!" whispered the officer giving the command.

"Fire!"

A volley rang out and was echoed through the surrounding forest. The elephant turned his head; blood was streaming from it. Then he rushed at the police, who continued to fire. He ignored the bullets and continued running. The police were by no means poor marksmen; they were simply not accustomed to the elephant anatomy, so their bullets failed to hit the brain and heart which are the elephant's most vulnerable parts. Trumpeting loudly with pain and fear, the elephant stretched out its trunk, only to roll it up quickly again: the trunk is a most important organ, without it the elephant quickly dies. For this reason the animal only uses it as a defence weapon or to attack in the most extreme cases. Hoity-Toity lowered his head and turned his enormous tusks like terrible battering rams against the enemy. Each tusk weighed about a hundred pounds. Only firm discipline kept the men at their posts, firing incessantly.

And yet the elephant broke through the cordon, smashed down the barricades and disappeared.

A chase was organized, but it was not at all easy to overtake him, let alone catch him. The police squads had to keep to the roads, but the elephant no longer picked his way; he stopped at nothing as he crossed gardens, orchards and forest-land.

IV. Wagner Saves the Situation

Meanwhile Strom was pacing his study in desperation.

"I'm ruined! Totally ruined!" he kept saying to himself. "My whole estate will have to go to pay for the damage the elephant has caused, and still they'll shoot Hoity-Toity. What an irretrievable loss it will be!"

Just then a servant handed Strom a message on a salver. "A cable for you," he said.

"That means it's all up!" thought the circus manager. "No doubt it's to say they've killed the elephant. But no, it's a cable from the Soviet Union! From Moscow!! Strange, who could have sent it?"

> "Manager Strom, Busch Circus, Berlin
> "Just read news item escape elephant stop request police immediately withdraw order to kill stop get a servant to give the following message to elephant colon quote sapiens comma wagner flying berlin stop return to busch circus stop unquote if he does not obey you then shoot him stop professor wagner."

Strom read the cable a second time.

"I don't understand! Evidently Professor Wagner knows the elephant. He uses his old name, Sapiens. But why does Wagner trust the elephant to return when he's told of the professor's arrival in Berlin? Still, the cable offers us a slim chance of saving the elephant."

The manager set to work. Only after some difficulty did he succeed in persuading the Chief of Police to "stop military operations." Jung was at once sent by aeroplane after the elephant.

Jung flourished a white kerchief in real truce envoy style as he approached Hoity-Toity.

"Most esteemed Sapiens!" he began. "Professor Wagner sends greetings. He is due to arrive in Berlin and wishes to see you. The Busch Circus will be the meeting-place. I assure you that if you return you will suffer no harm."

The elephant listened attentively, pondered for a moment, then picked Jung up in his trunk and set him on his back.

He then proceeded at a leisurely pace along the northward road to Berlin. Thus Jung found himself playing the role of both hostage and protector: with the man seated on the back of the elephant, no one dared to fire bullets.

The elephant plodded along on foot, of course; but Professor Wagner and Denisov, his assistant, flew to Berlin, and so arrived first. They immediately went to see Strom.

By this time the circus manager had received a telegram; it informed him that at the first mention of Professor Wagner, Hoity-Toity had become submissive and obedient and that he was now on his way back to Berlin.

"Would you mind telling me how you got the elephant and whether you know his history?" Wagner asked.

"I bought him from a trader of palm oil and nuts, by the name of Nix. He lives in the Congo, Central Africa, not far from Mathadi. He said the elephant turned up one day when his children were playing in the garden. He was performing all sorts of extraordinary tricks, standing on his hind legs, and dancing, juggling with sticks; at one point he thrust his tusks into the ground, stood on his front legs and waggled his hind legs and flourished his tail in a most comical way; Nix's children simply roared with laughter and rolled about on the grass. It was the children's idea to call the elephant Hoity-Toity, which everyone knows means 'playful, frisky' in English and is sometimes used as an interjection, something like 'Now, now!' The elephant grew accustomed to the name, and when he came to us we kept it. Here are the documents relating to the purchase. They're all in order, and no one can dispute the business deal."

"I don't intend disputing the deal," said Wagner. "Has the elephant any distinguishing marks?"

"There are some large scars on his head. Mr. Nix presumed they were from injuries caused when the elephant was captured. The natives have a pretty barbarous method of capturing elephants. The scars have disfigured him, and they might make the public feel uncomfortable, so we cover his head with a silk-embroidered cap with tassels."

"Then he is undoubtedly the identical elephant!"

"What do you mean?" asked Strom.

"He's Sapiens, the elephant I lost. I caught him during a scientific expedition into the Belgian Congo, and it was I who trained him. But one night he went off into the forest and didn't come back. We failed in all our efforts to find him."

"D'you mean you're laying claim to the elephant, then?" asked the circus manager.

"I'm not making any claim, but it is possible the elephant will. The fact is, I trained him by certain new methods which produce truly marvellous results. You've seen yourself the extraordinary development of the elephant's mental capacity. That was all my work. I would even say that Sapiens, or Hoity-Toity as you call him now, has the strongest sense of his own personality, if one can express it so. When I read in the newspapers of the marvellous ability shown by the elephant in your circus performances, I at once decided that my Sapiens alone was capable of such feats as reading, counting and even writing. For it was I who taught him all these things. So long as Hoity-Toity was living peacefully, affording pleasure to Berliners and obviously satisfied with his lot, I considered it was not necessary to interfere. But the elephant finally rebelled and that meant that something must have annoyed him. So I decided I must come to his aid. Now he must decide his fate for himself; he has the right to do so. Don't forget that if I had not arrived in time, the elephant would have been killed long ago; we should both have lost him. I only hope that you now realise that you will never compel the elephant by force to remain with you. But don't imagine that my sole purpose is to take him from you. I'll have a talk with him. It is possible that if you alter your system a bit, if you remove what has aggravated him so much, he will agree to stay with you."

"You'll have a talk with him! Whoever heard of such a thing!" exclaimed Strom, gesticulating wildly.

"There has never been anything like Hoity-Toity before," came the reply. "Incidentally, will he soon arrive in Berlin?"

"By this evening; he's evidently in a hurry to meet you. They telegraphed that he is coming at the rate of 15 miles an hour."

That very same evening, after the circus performance, Professor Wagner and Hoity-Toity met again. Strom, Wagner and Denisov were standing in the arena when the elephant entered from the artistes' passage, still carrying Jung on his back. The moment he caught sight of Wagner he hurried across to him, stretched out his trunk and gave Wagner a "handshake." He then removed Jung from his back, picked up Wagner and seated him there instead. The professor raised the elephant's huge ear and whispered something into it. The elephant nodded his head and began to wave the tip of his trunk rapidly before Wagner's face. Wagner closely watched these movements.

All this secrecy was not to Strom's taste.

"Come on, now," he said, impatiently. "What's the elephant decided?"

"He expresses a desire to take a vacation in order to have the opportunity of relating to me certain matters of interest. He agrees to return to the circus at the end of his holiday with one provision: that Herr Jung apologizes for rough-handling him and promises never again to use physical force. True, the elephant cannot feel the blows, but he is unprepared on principle to tolerate any kind of insult."

22

"You say I struck the elephant?" asked Jung, feigning surprise.

"With a broom-handle," replied Wagner. "You needn't be evasive, Jung; the elephant doesn't lie. You should be just as polite to the elephant as you would be to..."

"The President of the Republic, I suppose."

"...any human being who has any sense of dignity."

"A lord, perhaps?" said Jung, maliciously.

"That's quite enough of that!" cried Strom. "You're responsible for all the trouble, Jung, and I'll see you pay for it. When does Herr Hoity-Toity wish to take his vacation, and where?"

"We shall go on a walking tour with him," replied Wagner. "It will be most agreeable. His broad back will accommodate Denisov and myself, and he will carry us southwards. The elephant has expressed a desire to pasture in the Swiss meadows."

Assistant Denisov was still only twenty-three, but he had already made a number of biological discoveries in spite of his youth. "You'll go far," Wagner had told him when he took him to work in his laboratory. The young scientist had been delighted beyond description. The professor, too, had reason to be pleased with his assistant and wherever he went, Denisov went too.

"Denisov, Akim Ivanovich, these names are too long," Wagner had said the first day they worked together. "If I have to say Akim Ivanovich every time I address you I shall be spending 48 minutes a year on it. And a great deal could be done in that 48 minutes. So I shall avoid using any name unless I have to call you and then I shall yell out 'Den!', briefly and clearly. And you can call me Wag." Wagner was an adept at saving time.

By morning all was ready. There was ample room on the elephant's back for both Wagner and Denisov. Only essentials went with them.

In spite of the early hour, Strom was there to see them off.

"How will you feed the elephant?" he asked.

"We shall give performances in the towns and villages," Wagner replied. "In exchange, the spectators will give him food. Sapiens will feed us, as well as himself. Good-bye."

Slowly the elephant plodded down the street. But once they had left the last house behind and the highway lay ahead of the travellers, he increased the pace without being urged to. He proceeded at the rate of 7 miles an hour.

"It's your job to handle the elephant now, Den. And so that you will understand him, you must know about his rather unusual past. Just take this notebook; it's the diary kept by your predecessor, Peskov. He toured the Congo with me. Peskov had a tragicomic experience I'll tell you about one day. Meanwhile, read the diary."

Wagner shifted closer to the elephant's head, unfolded a small table and set it in front of himself, then began to write with both hands in two notebooks simultaneously. Wagner always did two operations at the same time.

"Come now, relate the whole story," he said, obviously to the elephant. The animal swung his trunk back till it almost reached Wagner's ear and began to make huffing noises very rapidly at brief intervals.

"Huff—ff—fff—f—ff—fff . . . ."

"Sounds like Morse Code," thought Denisov, as he opened a thick, oilcloth-bound exercise book.

With his left hand Wagner took down what the elephant dictated; with the right hand he wrote a scientific treatise. The elephant proceeded at a regular jog-trot and the smooth rocking motion scarcely interfered with his writing. Meanwhile Denisov quickly became absorbed in Peskov's diary. This is what he read.

V. "Ring Will Never Become a Man"

March 27. I feel as though I'm in Faust's study. Professor Wagner's laboratory is a marvellous place. It contains almost everything. Physics, chemistry, biology, electro-technology, microbiology, anatomy, physiology. . . . Apparently there is not a sphere of knowledge without its interest for Wagner, or Wag as he calls himself. Microscopes, spectroscopes, electroscopes, every imaginable "scope" for seeing what the naked eye alone cannot see. And a complete battery of hearing aids: ear "microscopes" with which Wagner can hear thousands of new sounds: "the underwater movement of sea serpents, the vegetative life of the distant vine." Glass, copper, aluminium, rubber, porcelain, ebony, platinum, gold, steel—all in a variety of forms and combinations. Retorts, flasks, coils, testtubes, lamps, spools, spirals, fuses, switches, buttons. . . . Can all this be a reflection of the complexity of Wagner's brain? Then in the adjoining room an entire waxworks exhibition. There Wagner "grows" human tissues, feeds the living finger detached from a human being, a rabbit's ear, a dog's heart, a sheep's head and . . . the brain of a man. A live, still thinking, human brain! It's my job to take care of it. To converse with it the professor presses a finger to the outer surface of the brain. And it is fed with some special physiological solution, and it's my business to make sure that it is always quite fresh. Some time ago Wagner changed the composition of this solution and began "intensive feeding" of the brain. The result was astounding! The brain began to grow very rapidly. I can't say it was a very handsome spectacle by the time it was the size of a large watermelon.

March 29. Wag has been having serious consultations with the brain about some matter or other.

March 30. This evening Wag said to me: "This is the brain of a young German scientist; his name was Ring. He died in Abyssinia, but, as you see, his brain still lives and can think. Lately, however, the brain has been somewhat saddened. It's not satisfied with the eye I made for it. It wants to hear as well as to see; it wants to move about, not to lie still all the time. Unfortunately, it's a little late announcing its desires. I might have been able to satisfy them, if only it had mentioned them before. I could have selected a cadaver in the anatomical theatre of suitable size; I could have put Ring's brain into its head. If the man had only died of some brain disease I could have brought him to life again by implanting a new, healthy brain in his head. Ring's brain would then have acquired a new body and the fullness of real life. But I concentrated on this tissue-growing experiment and now, as you see, Ring's brain has become so large that it won't fit any human skull. Ring will never become a man."

"Are you suggesting that Ring could become something other than a human being?"

"Just so. He can become an elephant, for example. True, his brain has not yet grown to the size of an elephant's brain, but that will come with time. We must only see to it that the brain assumes the required shape. I shall soon have an elephant's brain-box. I shall place the brain into it and continue to grow its tissues until they fill the entire cavity."

"Then, you're intending to make an elephant out of Ring?"

"Why not? I have already spoken to Ring about it. He has such a desire to see and hear, to move about and breathe, that he's ready to agree to become even a pig or a dog. But the elephant is a noble animal, strong, long-lived. And he may live, that is to say Ring's brain may live, another hundred or two hundred years. Is that such a poor prospect? Ring has already given his consent."

Denisov looked up from the diary to ask Wagner a question.

"I say, d'you mean to say the elephant we're now riding. . .?"

"Yes, yes, he has a human brain," replied Wagner without interrupting his writing. "Read on and don't bother me."

Denisov said no more but turned again to his reading. It seemed monstrous to him that the elephant on which they were riding had a human brain. He regarded the animal with a feeling of uncanny curiosity, almost superstitious horror.

March 31. Today the elephant brain-box arrived. The professor sawed longitudinally through the forehead.

"That's in order to put the brain in," he said, "and also so that it'll be convenient to remove it when we need to transfer it from this brain-box to another."

I examined the interior of the skull and was surprised at the comparatively small space the brain was required to fill. Externally the elephant gave the appearance of being far "brainier."

"Of all the land animals," Wag continued, "the elephant has the most highly developed frontal sinuses, see? The entire upper part of the skull consists of air chambers which the layman usually takes to be the brain-box. The brain itself is comparatively small and, in the elephant, is concealed far down, just about here; that would be approximately in the region of the ear. That's why shots directed at the front of the head don't usually reach the target: the bullets penetrate a few bone partitions, but do not destroy the brain."

Together we made a number of holes in the brain-box so that tubes could be passed through them for supplying the brain with nutritive solution; then we carefully fitted Ring's brain into one half of the brain-box. The brain by no means filled the cavity intended for it.

"Never mind, it'll grow during the journey," Wag assured me, fitting on the other half of the skull.

I must say I've very little faith in the success of Wag's experiment though I am quite aware of his numerous, extraordinary inventions. But this is an extremely complicated business. Tremendous obstacles have to be overcome. First it is essential for us to obtain a living elephant. It would be too expensive to have one sent from Africa or India. Then, for one reason or another, the elephant might turn out to be unsuitable. That's why Wag has decided to take Ring's brain to the Congo in Africa. He has been there before. There he will capture an elephant and carry out the brain-transplanting operation on the spot. The transplanting! It's easier said than done! It's nothing like transferring a pair of gloves from one pocket to another. All the nerve ends, the veins and arteries, have to be sorted out and stitched. The anatomy of a beast may be similar to that of a man, but there are still great differences. How will Wag manage to join these two different systems and make one of them? And the whole complicated operation has to be performed on a live elephant. . . .

VI. The Monkeys Play Football

June 27. Now the events of several days will have to be written up at one sitting. The journey provided a wealth of experiences and not all pleasurable ones. Already on the ship, and particularly in the tow-boat, we began to be besieged by mosquitoes. True, when we kept to the middle of the river, which was as broad as a lake, there were less of them. But we had only to get near the bank and we were at once enveloped in clouds of mosquitoes. Black flies clung to us and sucked our blood as we bathed. When we landed on the bank and set off on foot we were pursued by new enemies: small ants and sand-fleas. Every night we had to examine our feet and brush the fleas off them. Snakes, centipedes, bees and wasps all joined forces to trouble us.

It was no easy job penetrating the dense forest, yet it was scarcely less difficult walking out in the open. There the grasses stood twelve feet high and their stems were thick. It was like walking between two green walls and we couldn't see anything around us. It was horrible! The sharp blades of grass scratched our faces and hands. When we pressed down the grass it got tangled and twined round our legs. When it rained the water accumulated on the leaves and then showered down on us in bucketfuls. We had to march in single file along narrow paths through forests and over steppeland. Paths are the only ways of communication in those parts. There were twenty of us, eighteen being carriers and guides from one of the African tribes.

At last we reached our goal. We made a camp on the banks of lake Tumba. Our guides are now resting; in actual fact they are busy fishing. It is not easy to get them away from this occupation to help us to settle in. We have two large tents. The site chosen for the camp is a good one, on the side of a dry hill. The grass is not tall. We can see far into the distance all round us. Ring's brain travelled safely and is feeling pretty fair. It is impatiently waiting to return to the world of sounds, colours, scents and other sensations. Wag is comforting him with the thought that now he has not long to wait. He is engaged in some sort of mysterious preparations.

June 29. We're in a grand state of commotion: the natives have found some fresh tracks of a lion quite near to our camp.

I have unpacked the case of rifles and given one to each of the natives who declare they can shoot. After dinner we had shooting trials: it was something terrible! The natives press the rifle-butt to stomach or knee, turn somersaults on the recoil and the bullets fly off about 180° from the target. But their delight exceeds all bounds. Their shouting is incredible. I imagine their shouts will attract every ravenous beast in the Congo basin.

June 30. Last night the lion came quite close to the camp. He left material proof behind: he had torn a wild boar to pieces and devoured almost the whole of it. The boar's skull had been cracked like a nut, the ribs crunched into splinters. I don't fancy being caught in such a bone-crusher!

The natives are scared out of their wits. As soon as night falls they huddle together by our tents, light fires and keep the flames high all night. I've begun to understand primitive man's terror of the awful beast. When the lion roars—and I've heard it roaring several times—something just happens to me: the terror of distant ancestors stirs in my blood and my heart misses a beat. I feel I don't want to run away but just to sit hunched up or to dig myself into the earth like a mole. But Wag seems to be deaf to the lion's roaring. He is still in his tent, contriving something. After breakfast this morning he came out to me.

"Tomorrow morning I'm going into the forest," he said. "The natives say there's an old elephant track leading down to the lake. The elephants have been drinking not far from the camp. But they frequently change their pastures. The cutting they have made in the forest is already overgrown; that means they've gone off somewhere farther away. We've got to search them out."

"You realize, of course, that we've had a visit from a lion! So don't risk going without a rifle," I warned him.

"I'm not afraid of wild beasts," he replied. "I know how to exorcise them." His bushy moustache quivered as he tried to conceal a smile.

"Then you won't take a rifle with you?"

Wag merely shook his head.

July 2. In the interim some strange things happened. During the night the lion roared again; my stomach turned over, my heart went cold, I was so terrified. The following morning I was washing outside my tent when Wag emerged from the other one. He was wearing a white flannel suit, a cork helmet and strong, thick-soled boots: all dressed for an expedition. Yet he had neither rucksack nor rifle. I wished him good morning. He nodded a greeting and came forward, stepping, as it seemed to me, somewhat cautiously. Gradually his step became more confident and finally he was striding at his usual regular, rapid pace. He went on to the path which sloped down the hill and when it became really steep he raised his arms. It was then that something so strange happened that the natives and I cried out in surprise.

First of all his outstretched body began slowly whirling about in the air like a trapeze artiste; it continued in the same fashion, whirling faster and faster. One moment he was standing in a horizontal position, the next he was upside down with his feet in the air. He continued to describe circles as his legs and head exchanged positions until finally he was circling so fast that head and legs merged into one misty circle and his trunk resembled a dark nucleus. The whole business continued until Wag reached the bottom of the hill where, after somersaulting on level ground for a few yards, he straightened up and walked at his normal pace towards the forest.

I was absolutely mystified and the natives even more so. They were not just surprised, they were terrified. To them what they had seen was something supernatural. To me, this somersaulting was just one of the riddles that Wag was constantly confronting me with.

But riddles are all very well, what about the lion? Surely Wag was being over-confident this time. I know dogs are afraid of the supernatural: just try tying a string or horse hair to a bone and tossing it to a dog. Then, when the dog is just going to take the bone, tug gently on the string. When the bone moves across the ground as though escaping from the dog, the animal will tuck in its tail and hare away from what it imagines is a "live bone." But is a lion likely to do the same if it sees Wag somersaulting in the air? That's the question. I felt I could not leave Wag unprotected.

I grabbed a rifle and set off after him with four of the more courageous and intelligent of the natives. He was unaware of our presence as he strode forward along the fairly broad track the elephants had made in the forest. Thousands of beasts had trampled it down. In only one or two places did we encounter small, fallen tree trunks or dry twigs. But when Wag came to these obstacles, he hesitated, lifted his leg much higher than seemed necessary and with a strange movement took a long step over them. At one moment his body was inclined straightforward, not at all bent, the next he had straightened up again and proceeded on his way. We continued to follow him at some little distance. At last a bright patch of light appeared ahead of us, the path broadened and led us to a forest clearing.

Wag had already left the shade of the forest and was striding across the sunlit clearing when I heard a strange, low roaring or rumbling; it could only have come from a large beast that was angered or alarmed. But it did not resemble the roaring of a lion. The natives whispered the name of the beast, but I did not know the local names. Judging by the behaviour of my companions and the expressions on their faces, they were as much afraid of the growling beast as they were of the lion. But they kept close on my heels, while I quickened my pace, sensing danger. When I came out on the clearing a strange picture met my eyes.

About ten yards from the forest and to the right of me a baby gorilla about the size of a boy of ten was seated on the ground. Not far away was a greyish-brown female gorilla and a huge male. Wag was striding fairly rapidly across the level clearing and was obviously just between the baby gorilla and the parents before he noticed them. The male gorilla no sooner caught sight of Wag than he let out the same husky, growling sort of sound I had heard while still in the forest. By now Wag had seen the beasts; he advanced at his normal pace looking straight at the male gorilla. Then the young gorilla saw the man and quickly scrambled up a small tree near by, screeching and howling.

Again the male let out a warning sound. In general gorillas avoid man, but if they are forced into combat, they are most courageous and extraordinarily ferocious. The male gorilla noticed that the man was not retreating, and fearing for its young, suddenly stood up and assumed a belligerent posture. I doubt if there is a more terrible beast than this hideous likeness of man. For an ape, the male beast was enormous—as tall as a man of middle height, but with a chest expansion that seemed to be twice that of a man. The trunk was disproportionately large, the long arms as thick as logs. Hands and feet were extremely long. Under prominent overhanging brows, the eyes were fierce and enormous glistening teeth were bared in the snarling mouth.

The beast's hairy fists began to beat the chest so hard that it gave out a hollow sound like an empty barrel. Then it bellowed and whimpered, pushed off from the ground with its right hand and rushed at Wagner.

I must say I was so nervous that I couldn't get the rifle off my shoulder. By now the gorilla had covered the distance to Wag in no more than a few seconds and then ... again something most strange happened!

The ape knocked itself hard against some invisible obstacle, let out a yell and fell to the ground. On the contrary Wag, far from falling down too had somersaulted in the air like a trapeze artiste, his arms outstretched, his body raised to its full height. The ape's bad fortune heightened its fury. It scrambled up and tried to take a jumping leap at Wag. This time it went completely head over heels and again fell down. By now it was thoroughly infuriated; it bellowed and whimpered and foamed at the mouth; it hurled itself at Wag in an effort to grasp him in its tremendously long arms. But still an invisible but most reliable barrier lay between Wag and the gorilla. Judging by the position of the beast's arms, my guess was that the object was some sort of ball—invisible, transparent as glass, showing no high lights and strong as steel. So this was Wag's latest invention!

I was now convinced that Wag was perfectly safe, so I settled down to watch the extraordinary game with heightened interest. As the game became more lively, the natives danced with delight and even threw down their rifles.

For a while the female gorilla watched her frenzied partner with no less interest, apparently. Then she let out a belligerent howl and rushed to its assistance. From then on the game took on a different character. Excitedly the gorillas hurled themselves at the invisible ball which bounced from one spot to another like a regular football. It could have been no joke occupying a position inside the football while the gorillas behaved like excited footballers!

Wag whirled round and round like a catherine wheel; faster and faster, his body ever standing at attention, as it were. Now I could understand why he held his body so stiff and kept his arms extended. Both arms and legs were pressed against the inside wall of the ball to protect him from harm. The wall must be extraordinarily strong, for when the gorillas attacked it simultaneously from two sides, sending it upwards with a rush, it bounced up as much as three or more yards from the ground and still did not break when it came down. But Wag was beginning to tire. It is not possible to remain stretched out with the muscles tensed for very long. Suddenly I saw Wag double up and fall to the bottom of the ball.

Things had now taken a serious turn. We had to be more than spectators now. I cried out to the natives, made them pick up their rifles and together we moved towards the ball. I warned the natives not to shoot until I gave the order, fearing they might accidentally hit Wag. I was not sure whether the invisible ball was bullet-proof or not. Moreover, there must be some sort of opening in the ball, otherwise Wag would have been unable to breathe; a bullet might go through it.

We made a great deal of noise and shouting to draw attention to ourselves; and we succeeded. The male gorilla was the first to turn its head towards us; it growled menacingly. As this apparently made no impression on us, it began to come towards us. The moment it was out of the range of the ball, I fired. The bullet caught the gorilla in the chest; I saw blood trickling down the greyish-brown hair. The beast yelped and clapped a hand to the wound, but remained standing. Then it hurried faster towards me. I fired a second time, hitting it in the shoulder, by which time it was close to me and making a sudden grab at the barrel of my rifle. Its hand jerked the rifle from me with extraordinary force, it bent and broke the barrel before my eyes. As if this had not satisfied it, the gorilla bit at it and tried to gnaw it as though it were a bone. Then it staggered and dropped to the ground; its limbs twitched convulsively, though it was still clutching the mutilated rifle. The female gorilla meanwhile hurried back to shelter.

"Are you very much hurt?" said Wag, his voice seeming to come from some distance. Could I really have become hard of hearing just because a gorilla had brushed against my side?

I looked up and saw Wag standing over me. Now that he was close I could see a sort of cloudy membrane round his body. Peering more closely I realized that it was not the actual membrane I could see, for it was absolutely transparent; but prints from the gorilla's hands and patches of dirt were clinging to the surface of the ball.

Wag must have noticed me staring at these patches on the invisible ball.

"When the soil is damp or muddy," he explained with a smile, "it leaves patches on the surface and the ball becomes visible. But sand and dry leaves don't stick to it. If you're feeling strong enough, pick yourself up and let's turn back. On the way I'll explain my invention."

I rose to my feet and looked closely at Wagner. He, too, had suffered a little; there were bruises on his face.

"That's nothing, it's a mere scratch! This has all been a lesson to me. It seems one cannot penetrate the thickets of the African forest even in a ball as impenetrable as this, unless one takes a rifle as well. Who would have thought I'd ever find myself inside a football!"

"So the comparison did strike you?"

"Certainly. Now, listen here. Did you ever read about the metal the Americans have invented that's as transparent as glass? Or of the glass that is as strong as metal? It's said that it's used to build army planes. Its advantages are obvious:

it's almost invisible to the enemy. I say almost because the pilot must be just as visible as I am through my ball. Well, for a long time I toyed with the idea of building a sort of 'fortress,' through which I could see everything. I could observe animal life, but the 'fortress' would protect me if wild beasts caught sight of me and attacked me. I made a number of experiments and finally reached my goal. This particular ball is made of rubber. Aha! people have by no means exhausted all the possibilities of this extremely useful material. I have succeeded in making rubber as transparent as glass and as strong as steel. In spite of our rather unpleasant adventure today, which might have ended even more unpleasantly if you had not come to my aid in the nick of time, I consider the invention most successful and expedient. As for the gorillas, who would have thought I'd encounter them here? True, it's rather a wild spot, but gorillas usually inhabit the wilder, impenetrable thickets."

"But how do you get about from one place to another?"

"Oh! quite simply. Don't you see? I step on the inside wall of the ball and the weight of my body pushes the ball forward. There are breathing holes on the surface of the ball, which is made in two half-sections. When I've entered it, I shut myself in by tugging at a special strap made of transparent rubber. I must say the drawback is that it is difficult to restrain the ball on slopes; it starts rolling so fast that I am forced to do physical jerks! But why not?"

VII. Invisible Fetters

July 20. Another break in my diary. The elephants seem to have gone very far afield. We had to strike camp and follow the track for several days before we finally picked up fresher traces of the herd. But two days later the natives found the elephants' water-hole. The natives are experienced elephant-hunters and use numerous methods to capture them. But Wag preferred his own, original methods. He had ordered a crate to be brought along, and now he took something invisible from it. The natives looked on in superstitious horror while Wag's hands went through the motions of lifting things out and laying them aside, although the "things" he handled were as invisible as air. The natives probably regarded Wagner as a superior kind of sorcerer.

Wag had said nothing to me, but I had already guessed he was unpacking some sort of contrivance for capturing elephants and that he had made it from the same invisible material as had been used to make the ball.

"Come over and feel it," invited Wagner, seeing that I was burning with curiosity.

I went over and fumbled about in the air until my hands closed on a rope about a centimetre thick.

"Is it rubber?"

"Yes, one of the innumerable varieties of rubber. For this particular purpose I've made it as flexible as rope. But it has the same steel-like strength and invisibility as the ball. We'll make nooses out of these invisible ropes and set them in the path of the elephants. We'll catch one of them, and then we'll have full control of it."

I must say it was not an easy job laying the invisible ropes on the ground and tying nooses. Time and again we caught a foot in a rope and stumbled. But by nightfall the work was finished; we had nothing left to do but wait for the elephants.

It was a splendid tropical night. The jungle was filled with rustlings and sighings and at times there were sounds like the cries of a small creature departing this life. Sometimes wild peals of laughter rang out, while the natives huddled closely together as though they had been doused with cold water.

Imperceptibly the elephants approached. The enormous leader was a little ahead of the herd, its trunk stretched forward and in continual motion. It was feeling the thousands of nocturnal scents, classifying them, making a mental note of the scents that spelled danger. When only a few yards from our invisible nooses, the animal pulled up sharply, its trunk stretched straighter than I had ever before seen. It was concentrating on some scent or other. Perhaps it was the smell of our bodies although, on the advice of the natives, we had all bathed in the lake and washed our clothing just before sundown. One sweats all day long at the Equator.

"That's bad," whispered Wag. "The elephant has scented our presence; I imagine it has got wind of the rubber, not our bodies. I overlooked that possibility."

The elephant was clearly hesitating, trying to accustom itself to a smell that was new to it. What sort of danger was connected with this unfamiliar smell? Hesitatingly it advanced a little, perhaps to make a closer investigation of the source of the strange smell. A few more paces, and it was caught in the first noose. Its foreleg tugged, but the invisible fetter clung fast. The animal dragged harder on the rope; we saw the pressure on the skin just above the foot. Then the huge animal pulled its whole body back, so that its hind quarters almost touched the ground. The pressure from the rope cut the skin through the great thickness of elephant hide, and thick, dark blood trickled down the leg.

Wagner's rope could evidently take an extraordinary amount of strain.

We were already celebrating our victory when the unforeseen occurred. The thick tree trunk, to which the rope was attached, cracked as though an axe had been at it. The elephant, taken by surprise, fell back, quickly stumbled to its feet again, then turned and made off, trumpeting its alarm.

"That's torn it!" muttered Wag. "The elephants won't come near places where we lay our invisible nooses; they can sense them by the smell. I'll have to get down to some chemical deodorizing. Chemical ... hm ... smells ... just so...." Wagner was plunged in thought. Then he went on: "And why not? You see what I have in mind: we could try chemical means of capturing an elephant, a gas attack, for instance. We needn't kill the elephant; that would be easy enough to do. We have to make it unconscious. We'll wear gas-masks; take a drum of gas with us and let it off on this same forest track. The surrounding vegetation is very dense; in fact it's an absolute tunnel of vegetation; the gas will keep in pretty well. And then ... but there's an even simpler method!"

Suddenly Wagner burst out laughing; something had evidently tickled his fancy.

"Now all we have to do is to find out where the elephants go for water. They're hardly likely to return to this spot ...."

VIII. Vodka for Elephants

July 21. The natives have found another water-hole, a tiny forest lake. As soon as the animals had finished drinking and gone off into the thicket, Wag and I set to work with the natives to help us. We stripped, went into the water and began knocking wooden piles into the bottom, closely together in a row to barricade off a small part of the lake. Then we plastered the underwater wall with a thick layer of clay. This made us a sort of breeding-pond. The dam enclosed that part of the lake where the elephants had been seen to drink.

"That's magnificent!" exclaimed Wag. "Now all we have to do is 'poison' the water. I've an excellent, perfectly harmless method of doing it; it acts better than alcohol."

For several hours Wag worked in his laboratory; finally he

brought out a bucketful of what he called "elephant vodka." The liquid was poured into the pond. Meanwhile we all climbed trees and settled down to take observations.

"But will the elephants drink the vodka?" I asked.

"I'm only hoping they'll find it tasty. After all, bears like vodka; in fact they've been known to become regular drunkards. Sh! Something's coming."

I looked round the "arena," which was very large.

But here I will diverge a little, because I should mention that I never ceased to be astonished at the picturesque nature and "architectural" variety of the tropical forest. From time to time one finds oneself passing through a "three-tiered" forest: a little area of scrub and low trees scarcely higher than a man; above this—a second forest with trees roughly as high as those in our own northern forests; finally, rising higher still, a third forest of huge trees. Between the tops of the first and second rows of trees was an area of ropes and cables from all kinds of climbing plants. A three-tiered forest of this kind is an amazingly beautiful sight! High overhead the green caves, green waterfalls tumbling in cascades, green-blue mountains disappearing skywards, and the whole splashed with the brightly coloured plumage of birds, the exquisite colours of orchids.

Sometimes one suddenly finds oneself in something like a magnificent gothic cathedral, a forest of gigantic columns rising from the mossy earth to a scarcely visible dome. Then, a few steps farther on, everything is transformed: a labyrinth of impenetrable thicket. Leaves to the left, leaves to the right, leaves in front, behind and overhead. Moss, grasses, leaves and flowers below, reaching shoulder high. It was like floundering in a green whirlpool, legs entangled in lush vegetation, feet stumbling against fallen trees. When one is almost worn out and apparently in a hopeless confusion of dense undergrowth, the scrub recedes and one stands transfixed. a green, vaulted, circular cave, its vast dome supported by a "column" of incredible dimensions. There is no grass at all underfoot for a croquet-lawn. The undergrowth has been killed by the shade from one gigantic tree which cuts off every ray of the sun. The tree's branches droop down to the ground and have taken root there. The light in the cave is dim, and it is cool. Often we rested in the shade of these giants, the rubber trees and Indian fig-trees.

To continue my story. It was just such a gigantic tree that was now sheltering us in its branches. It stood quite close to the lake and every wild beast using the elephant track had to pass across the "arena" to reach the bank. Many a forest drama had apparently been enacted on this "arena": here and there lay the picked bones of antelope, buffalo and wild boar. The savannahs were not far distant and animals frequently came in from there to drink.

A wild boar crossed the "arena," followed by a female and eight young. The entire family trooped down to the water. A moment later five more female beasts appeared, evidently from the same herd. The boar approached the water and began to drink. In a moment it had raised its snout, snorted disapprovingly and moved to another spot. It tried the water again, showed displeasure and shook its head.

"It won't drink," I whispered to Wag.

"It's got to acquire the taste," he replied.

And he was right. Soon the boar stopped shaking its head and began drinking steadily. But the female boar was disturbed and it seemed to me that it was warning its young not to drink. But it soon acquired a taste for the water: for a very long time, longer than is customary, the boars and their young drank from the lake. The young were the first to feel the effects; they began squealing and pouncing on each other and rushing round the "arena." Next, all six female beasts began to stagger and behave peculiarly, squealing and bucking, rearing and bristling, rolling on the ground, even turning somersaults. At last they dropped to the ground and were sleeping soundly with their young. But intoxication roused the boar and it became turbulent. It grunted fiercely, rushed at the huge tree trunk in the centre of the "arena"; it plunged its stiletto tusks with such force into the bark that it had difficulty in extricating them.

We were so absorbed in the antics of the intoxicated boar that we failed to notice the elephants approaching. Slowly they came, with measured tread, from the green track. They were advancing in single file. Then, indeed, did the area round the tree trunk resemble a regular circus arena. But never did a circus witness such a large number of four-legged artistes. I have to admit that the sight of so many of them terrified me. They looked like enormous rats, more than two dozen of them!

But the antics of the wild, drunken boar were not at all what one would have imagined! Instead of turning tail while it still had its skin intact, it grunted menacingly and rushed swift as an arrow at the herd of elephants. The lead elephant was obviously taken aback, for it stared curiously at the onrushing brute, which plunged its tusk into the elephant's leg. But the elephant swiftly rolled up its trunk, lowered its head and struck the boar such a blow with its tusks, that it was flung the whole of the distance to the lake. The boar grunted and floundered; it scrambled to the bank, contriving on the way to swallow a few mouthfuls to give itself courage, as it were; then it again rushed at the elephant. But this time the latter showed more caution: it was waiting for the boar with its tusks lowered. As the boar rushed on, the elephant's tusks pierced deeply into its body. The elephant shook the dying beast from its tusks and brought one foot down on it. Of the boar, all that remained was its head and tail; the body was crushed flat.

Calmly and at a regular pace the lead elephant picked its way across the "arena" as though nothing had happened; it avoided the bodies of the female boars and their young lying deeply oblivious to everything on the ground. It reached the water and plunged its trunk into the lake. Our curiosity was heightened as we watched to see what would happen.

The elephant took a draught of water, raised its trunk to the surface and began to fumble about with it, evidently comparing the taste of the water in different parts of the lake. It took a few steps and dropped its trunk into the water beyond the partition we had made. There the water was not contaminated by our intoxicating liquid.

"Now the game's up!" I whispered. But the words were hardly out of my mouth than I almost let out a yelp of surprise. The elephant had returned to the first spot and was drinking the "elephant vodka!" It seemed to prefer it. The others lined up beside their lead elephant. Our dam was not very large, consequently some of the herd drank pure, fresh water.

I thought they would never stop drinking. I could see that the lead elephant's sides had swollen enormously as it went on drinking. Half an hour later the level of our pond had dropped by fifty per cent. An hour later the lead elephant and its companions were sucking up what remained of the liquid at the bottom. Even before they had finished, they began tottering about. One of them collapsed in the water, causing a great commotion. It trumpeted, rose to its feet and fell on its side a second time. With its trunk lying on the bank, it set up such a snoring that the leaves trembled and the scared birds flew up to the tree-tops.

Snorting loudly, the lead elephant moved away from the

lake, its trunk hung down as limp as a rag. For a moment it raised its ears, only to let them drop again, seemingly lifeless. It rocked to and fro, slowly and rhythmically. All round lay its companions, as though mown down by bullets. The elephants that had failed to get any "vodka" surveyed the strange "losses" in their ranks with an air of surprise. These sober elephants trumpeted with concern, walked round and round the "drunkards" and even tried to raise them up. One large female elephant approached the leader and showed its concern by touching its head with her trunk. The elephant wagged its tail feebly in response to this gesture of kindness and sympathy, but continued its regular, rocking motions. Then suddenly it raised its head, let out a loud snore, and dropped to the ground. The sober elephants, quite at a loss, crowded round it; they hesitated to depart without the lead elephant.

"It'll be awkward if the sober ones decide to remain," said Wag, now speaking aloud. "We'd have to kill them, wouldn't we? Let's wait a bit and see what happens next."

The sober elephants went into some sort of conference, making strange noises and waving their trunks about. This continued for a little time. The setting sun was turning the sky crimson by the time the elephants had selected a new leader and slowly filed singly out of the "arena" where lay the "corpses" of their companions.

IX. Ring Becomes an Elephant

The time had come to descend from the tree. Apprehensively I surveyed the "arena" which now resembled a battlefield. The huge elephants, with wild boars in between, lay on their sides. Would this drunken state last long? Suppose the elephants sobered up before we'd finished the brain-transplanting operation? As though to augment my fear, the elephants flourished their trunks from time to time and squealed in their sleep.

But Wag was oblivious to all this. Swiftly he descended the tree and set to work. While the natives occupied themselves killing off the sleeping boars, Wag and I performed the operation. Everything had been prepared in readiness. Wag had ordered surgical instruments of a kind that could be used on the hardness of ivory. He went up to the elephant, selected a sterilised scalpel from the case, made an incision in the elephant's head, turned back the skin and began to saw through the skull. Once or twice the elephant's trunk twitched, which made me feel very nervous. Wag comforted me.

"There's no need to feel alarmed. I can guarantee the efficacy of my narcotic. The elephant will remain asleep for three hours, by which time I hope to have its brain out. After that it will not be a danger to us."

He continued to saw methodically through the skull. The instruments were indeed excellent; soon he lifted off part of the parietal bone.

"Should you ever go hunting elephants," he said, "remember just this: you can only kill an elephant by hitting it in this tiny little spot." Wag pointed to a space not larger than the palm of a hand situated between the eye and the ear. "I've already warned Ring's brain to take great care of this spot."

Wag had soon removed the brainy substance from the elephant's head. But then the unexpected happened. The brainless elephant moved a little and rocked its ponderous body; finally to our immense surprise it got up and walked a few paces. It could obviously see nothing in front of it, even though its eyes were open; it made no attempt to avoid its companions lying in its path and so stumbled and fell again to the ground. Its trunk and legs began to twitch convulsively.

"Is it dying?" I thought, regretting that all the labour had been in vain.

Wag merely waited until the elephant had stopped moving and then resumed the operation.

"The elephant is now dead," he remarked, "just like any animal without a brain. But we shall resurrect it. It's not difficult to do. Pass me Ring's brain, quickly.... Let's hope no infection has got in!"

After carefully washing my hands I took Ring's brain out of the elephant skull we had brought with us and passed it to Wag.

"There you are!" he said, lowering the brain into the skull.

"Does it fit?" I asked.

"It's a trifle small. But that's of no consequence. It would have been worse if it had grown too large to fit the brain-box. Now for the most important part—sewing up the nerve ends. Each nerve I join will make contact between Ring's brain and the body of the elephant. You can take a rest now. Just sit and watch, but don't hinder me."

Wag set to work with extreme speed and care. Indeed, he was an artist and his fingers worked like those of a virtuoso performing a most difficult work on the piano. His expression was concentrated, both eyes were fixed on one spot, as they always were when he had to devote exceptional attention to his work. Obviously both sides of his brain were carrying out the same work, acting as controls to each other, as it were. Finally he fitted the cranium over the brain, fastened it together with metal clips, laid the skin in position and put in the stitches.

"Excellent! Now, if it heals properly, there'll be nothing to show but the scars on the skin. But I think Ring will excuse me for that."

Ring will excuse him! Of course, the elephant was now Ring

47

or, rather, Ring had become an elephant. I moved closer to the elephant with the human brain in its head; I looked with curiosity into its open eyes. They still looked just as lifeless as before.

"What's the explanation?" I asked. "Ring's brain should be fully conscious, yet the eyes (I couldn't bring myself to say the elephant's, or Ring's) appear to be glassy."

"It's quite simple," replied Wag. "The nerves running from the brain have been stitched, but they haven't yet grown together. I warned Ring not to try to make any movements until the nerve-ends have completely grown together. I have done everything possible to ensure that this happens as quickly as possible."

Already the sun was beginning to set. The natives, seated on the bank of the lake, were roasting wild boar's flesh over their fire and eating the meat with relish. Some of them even preferred eating it raw. Suddenly one of the drunken elephants began trumpeting. The sharp call wakened the others and they all began to get on their legs. Followed by the natives, Wag and I hurried to take cover in the bushes. The elephants were still tottery; they went up to the lead elephant, still sleeping after the operation; their trunks felt him over and sniffed at him, they conversed in their own animal language. I can just imagine how Ring would have felt if he had been able to see and hear. At last the elephants went away, and we approached our patient again.

"Keep silent and don't reply to me," said Wag to the elephant, just as though he could talk. "I can only allow you to blink your eyelid, if you have the strength to do so. Now. If you can understand what I am saying, blink twice."

The elephant blinked.

"That's very good!" said Wag. "Today you will have to lie still, but I may let you get up tomorrow. We shall barricade the elephant track so that elephants and other wild beasts won't disturb you; we shall light fires during the night."

July 24. Today the elephant got up for the first time.

"Congratulations!" Wag greeted him. "What shall we call you now? We mustn't publicise your secret. I'll call you Sapiens, do you agree?"

The elephant gave a nod.

"We shall converse in mime or Morse code," continued Wag. "You can wave the end of your trunk: upwards for a dot, sideways for a dash. Or if you find it more convenient you can make sound signs. Wave your trunk now."

The elephant proceeded to wave his trunk, but rather awkwardly: it seemed to swing in all directions like a dislocated limb.

"You're not used to it yet. You see, Ring, you've never had a trunk before. But let's see how you can walk."

The elephant began to walk; the hind legs seemed to obey him better than the forelegs.

"I see you'll have to learn to be an elephant," was Wag's comment. "There's not much of the elephant brain in yours. But you'll pretty soon learn to move your legs, trunk and ears. Of course, the elephant's instincts are inborn; they are the quintessence of the experience of hundreds of thousands of generations of elephants. A real elephant knows what it has to fear, how to protect itself against different enemies, where to find food and water. You have no knowledge of such things. You will have to learn by experience, the sort of experience for which many elephants have paid with their lives. But you mustn't be dismayed or fearful, Sapiens. We shall be with you all the time. As soon as you have quite recovered, we'll all go to Europe together. If you wish, you can live in your native land, Germany; or you can come with us back to the Soviet Union. There you will live in the Zoological Gardens. But tell me, how are you feeling now?"

It transpired that Sapiens-Ring found it easier to make signs by means of a gentle puffing than by making trunk movements. He began making long and short puffing sounds through his trunk. Wag listened and translated for me (I did not understand the Morse code in those days).

"My sight doesn't seem to be as good as it was. It's true I can see farther, as I'm taller; but the field of vision is rather restricted. The hearing and sense of smell are amazingly subtle and keen. I never imagined there were so many sounds and smells in the world. I can smell thousands of new, strange scents and nuances. I can hear countless numbers of sounds for which probably no words exist in the human language. Whistling, crackling, squeaking, chirruping, squealing, groaning, barking, shouting, rumbling, clattering, clanking, crunching, slapping, clapping and perhaps a dozen or so additional words, and the number of words expressing sounds is completely exhausted. But beetles and grubs boring into the bark of trees, for instance, how can that discordant concert which I hear so clearly be conveyed in words? And all the noises!"

"You're progressing, Sapiens," commented Wag.

"And all the other scents!" continued Sapiens-Ring, describing his new sensations. "Here I am, quite at a loss to convey to you even an approximation of what I can sense. All you can understand is that every tree, every object has its own specific smell." The elephant lowered its trunk to the ground and sniffed. "See, the earth smells," he continued. "And it smells of the grass lying here that was dropped, perhaps, by some herbivorous animal on its way to the water. It smells of wild boar, buffalo, copper... ! I can't imagine where that smell came from. Ah! yes, here's a scrap of copper wire that you most likely dropped, Wagner."

"How can this be?" I asked. "The subtlety of the senses is not merely determined by the subtlety of the peripheral receiving organs, but also by the corresponding brain development."

"Yes," replied Wag. "When Ring's brain is, as it were, completely accustomed, it will possess senses which are as subtly perceptive as those of an elephant. So far his senses are probably several times less subtly perceptive than those of a real elephant. But Ring's subtle auditory and olfactory apparatuses are already giving him a tremendous advantage over us." He turned to the elephant. "I'm hoping it will not be too burdensome for you, Sapiens, if we travel back to the hill camp on your back."

Sapiens benevolently agreed to the proposal and nodded his head. We loaded part of the baggage on to his back and in his trunk he lifted Wagner and me and put us on his back, too. Off we went, the natives following on foot.

"I think Sapiens will be perfectly well in a couple of weeks; then he will carry us to Bom, and from there we shall travel home by sea."

We set up our camp on the hill.

"There's plenty of fodder for you here," said Wag to Sapiens. "But please don't go too far from the camp, particularly at night. There may be all kinds of danger lurking for you, which a real elephant, of course, could easily cope with."

The elephant nodded and began to use his trunk to break off the branches of nearby trees.

Suddenly he squealed, rolled up his trunk and hurried to Wag.

"What's up?" asked Wag. The elephant thrust his trunk almost into Wag's face.

"Dear me!" exclaimed Wag, reproachfully. He called me over and pointed to the finger-like end of the elephant's trunk. "This little finger is more sensitive than the fingers of a blind man In fact, it's the elephant's most sensitive organ Look here, our Sapiens has contrived to prick his finger on a thorn."

Gently Wag removed the thorn, then cautioned the elephant.

"Now, you've got to be very careful. An elephant with an injured trunk is an invalid. You'll find you can't even drink water, then you'll have to go down to the river or lake whenever you're thirsty and drink through your mouth instead of using your trunk, as elephants do, and pouring the water into your mouth. There are lots of prickly plants here. Search a little farther away; you'll soon learn to distinguish the different species."

Sighing heavily the elephant rolled up his trunk again and walked towards the forest.

July 27. Everything is going well. The elephant eats an incredible amount of food. At first he was particular about what he ate and only stuffed grass, leaves and the thinnest, tenderest twigs into his mouth. But as he never seemed satisfied, he soon began breaking down branches as thick as an arm and stuffing them into his mouth like a real elephant.

The trees round the camp are a pitiable sight: just as though a meteorite had fallen or a horde of all-consuming locusts had flown in. There's not a leaf left in the undergrowth and on the lower branches of the taller trees. The twigs are broken or stripped off, the bark torn away, the ground strewn with litter: dung, bits of twigs, trunks of small felled trees. Sapiens is eternally apologising for all the destruction but "circumstances compel it," as he transmitted to Wag through his sound signals.

August 1. This morning Sapiens didn't put in an appearance. At first Wagner was not at all perturbed.

"He's hardly a needle in a haystack. We'll find him all right. After all, what could happen to him? There's not a beast who would dare to attack him. He probably went far afield during the night."

The hours passed and there was no sign of Sapiens. Finally we decided to send out a search party for him. The natives are excellent trackers and they quickly picked up the trail. We followed behind them. One old native kept up a running commentary on the tracks the elephant had left by merely looking at the trail he had left behind.

"Here the elephant ate some grass, there he began eating the young scrub. Here he seems to have taken a jump, something must have scared him: the trail of a leopard. Another jump, and just here the elephant began running, crashing through everything in his path. And the leopard? It ran too . . . away from the elephant, exactly in the opposite direction."

The elephant's trail led us far away from the camp. Here he had hurried across a swampy field, there was water in the footprints he had left. The elephant had sunk into the mire but continued to run, with difficulty dragging his feet out of the swamp. Then we found ourselves at the river, the Congo. The elephant had plunged into the water in order to swim to the opposite bank.

Our guides set off to find a native village; there they obtained a boat and we crossed to the opposite bank; but we could pick up no tracks. Could Sapiens have drowned? Elephants can swim, but could Ring? Had he managed to master the art of swimming elephant-fashion? The natives suggested that the elephant had swum downstream. For several miles we floated down on the current. Still we found no sign of the elephant. Wag grew despondent. All our labours had been in vain. And what, indeed, had become of the elephant? Even if he were alive, how would he manage to live with the other beasts of the forest?

August 8. We spent a whole week searching for the elephant but all in vain! He has vanished, leaving no trace. We can do nothing now but pay off the natives and return home.

X. Hostile Quadrupeds and Bipeds

"Well, I've finished reading the diary," announced Denisov.

"All right; here's the continuation," replied Wag, patting the elephant's neck. "While you've been reading, Sapiens alias Hoity-Toity alias Ring has been relating the interesting story of his adventures. I'd given up all hope of seeing him alive again, but it appears he was quite able to find his own way back to Europe. You must decipher my shorthand note of the story and type it out for me."

Denisov took the exercise-book from Wagner. It was peppered with dashes and commas. Slowly he started reading, then writing out, the history of adventures the elephant had related himself. This is what Sapiens told Wagner:

I can hardly hope to convey to you all I have experienced since becoming an elephant. Never in my wildest dreams did I ever imagine that I, Professor Turner's assistant, would suddenly become transformed into an elephant and spend part of my life in the thickets of the African forest. I will try to outline the course of events consecutively.

I had not gone far from the camp and was peacefully pulling up grass in a meadow. I pulled it up in whole clumps, shook it to get the clinging soil off the roots and then chewed the succulent grass. When I had had my fill of the grass, I went on into the forest in search of more pasture-land. It was a fairly bright, moonlit night. Fire beetles, bats and unfamiliar nocturnal birds like owls were flying all round. Slowly I went forward. I found it easy going and was not conscious of the weight of my body. I tried to make as little noise as possible. Through my trunk I caught the wind of wild beasts to the right and left of me, but I did not know what kind they were. I felt as though nothing could frighten me. I am stronger than all the other wild beasts. Even the lion should defer to me. And yet, every slight rustle, every little noise of a scurrying mouse, of some little creature like a fox, seemed to scare me. When I met a small boar, I stood aside to let it pass. Perhaps I was still not fully conscious of my strength. But one thing comforted me: I knew there were people not far away, that I had friends ever ready to come to my aid.

So, stepping carefully, I came to a small clearing. I was about to lower my trunk to pull up a bunch of grass when I suddenly caught the wind of a wild beast and my ears heard the sound of rustling among some rushes. I raised my trunk, carefully rolled it up for safety and began to look about me. Suddenly I caught sight of a leopard lurking in the rushes by a stream; it was glaring at me out of greedy, ravenous eyes. Its body was tense, ready to spring. Another minute and he would have leapt to my neck. I cannot say why I did it, perhaps I was still not accustomed to being an elephant and was feeling and reasoning too much like a human being. I couldn't control an insane feeling of terror and I took to flight, trembling all over.

Trees crashed and fell in my path. Several wild beasts took fright as I madly rushed away. They darted out of bushes and grass, fleeing in all directions and heightening my own fear. I felt I was being chased by every wild beast in the Congo. I don't know how long I stampeded or where I was running to, but at length I was brought up sharply by an obstacle—the river. I cannot swim or, rather, I couldn't swim when I was a man. Still, the leopard was after me I thought and so I plunged into the river and began to work my legs as though I was still running. I found myself swimming. The water cooled me down and I began to feel calmer. But I still had the sensation that the entire forest was full of hungry wild beasts ready to fall upon me the moment I set foot on the bank. So on and on I swam, hour after hour. The sun had already risen and I was still swimming. Boats appeared on the river carrying people, but I was not afraid of people; not until I heard a shot ring out from one of the boats. It did not enter my head that they were firing at me, so I went on swimming. Then a second shot rang out and suddenly I felt as though a bee had stung me on the back of the neck. I turned my head and saw a white man, dressed like an Englishman, sitting in the boat the natives were rowing. He was the person firing at me. Alas! It seemed that people were just as harmful to me as the wild beasts!

What then could I do? I wanted to shout to the Englishman to hold his fire, but could only make a sort of squeaking sound. Once the Englishman hit his target, I would be dead. You remember you told me about the vulnerable spot—between the eye and ear—where the brain was situated. I remembered your advice and turned my head to prevent the bullets from hitting this spot, while I made for the bank at full speed. I made an excellent target as I clambered up the bank, but my head was at least turned towards the forest.

Meanwhile, the Englishman was evidently so well acquainted with the rules of big game hunting that he decided it was futile to shoot at my rump. He held his fire, probably waiting to see if I would turn and face him. But I hurried off into the thicket with no more thought about wild beasts.

The forest grew denser and denser. Lianas barred my way and I was soon so entangled in them that I could not tear them away and had to call a halt. I was so dead tired that I fell on my side caring little whether or not, being an elephant. this was really the sort of thing to do.

And then I had a terrible dream. I dreamed I was a university lecturer, Professor Turner's assistant. I was in my little study in Unter den Linden, Berlin. It was a fine summer night; one lone star was shining through the open window. The scent of the lime trees wafted in from outside; on the little table stood some sweetly-scented red carnations in a blue Venetian glass vase. Among these pleasing scents there came, like an uninvited guest, a sharp, sickly-sweet smell, something like black-currants, which I recognized, however, as the smell of a wild beast. At the time I was preparing for the following day's lecture. My head was bent over my books; then I dozed for a while, still conscious however of the scent of limes, carnations and wild beasts. Then I had another terrible dream: that I had become an elephant and was in a tropical forest. The smell of wild beasts grew stronger and disturbed me. I woke up, or so it seemed to me. But this was not a dream. I really had become an elephant, just as Lucius had become an ass,* only in my case it was because of the magic of modern science.

I caught the wind of a two-legged animal, the smell came from the sweat of an African native. Mingled with it was the smell of a white man. He was probably the man who had fired at me from the boat. Then he was on my trail again! Perhaps he was already standing hidden behind a bush, the barrel of his gun trained on the little spot between the eye and ear.

I jumped up quickly. The smell came from the right-hand side, then I must make off to the left. And so I ran, breaking down bushes and pushing them aside. And then—without knowing who had taught me the trick—I behaved as elephants

---

¹ Lucius—hero of Apuleius' *The Golden Ass*.

do when they want to put the pursuer off the trail. After making a noisy retreat, the elephant becomes perfectly still and quiet. The pursuer, hearing no sound at all, thinks the elephant has stopped in its tracks. But actually the elephant is still fleeing, only he is stepping very cautiously, moving the branches so very gently that even a cat, stealthy as it is, could not emulate it.

I ran on for as much as two miles before I finally summoned up enough courage to turn and sniff the air. I could still scent people, but they were as much as a mile away, I reckoned. I continued my flight.

The tropical night came down, stifling, intensely hot and dark as blindness. With the darkness my terrors returned. They enveloped me on all sides and were as infinite as the darkness. Where could I flee to for safety? What could I do? It seemed more terrible to remain still than to move on. So at a steady, indefatigable pace I pressed on.

Soon my feet were splashing through water. A few more steps, and I was standing on a bank. The bank of what? A river? A lake? I decided to swim again. In the water I could at least feel safe from any attack from lions and leopards. I swam on until, to my surprise, I found myself standing on the bottom, in shallow water. I continued to walk on.

I encountered streams, small rivers and swamps in my path. Small, unseen creatures hissed at me from the grass; huge frogs hopped fearfully aside. Throughout the night I wandered on and by morning I had to admit that I was completely lost.

After a few more days had passed I ceased to be afraid of much of what had previously filled me with terror. It was strange, but during the first few days of my new existence I had even been afraid of the prickles hurting my skin. Perhaps the incident of the thorn in the finger of my trunk had given me cause to fear. However, soon I discovered that even the sharpest, toughest prickles did not harm me at all, for my tough skin protected me like armour. In the early days I had been afraid of accidentally stepping on a poisonous snake. And the first time this happened and the snake twined itself round my leg trying to bite me, my huge elephant heart had turned cold with fear. But I soon realized that the snake is powerless to harm me. Since then I have even taken some pleasure in crushing underfoot any snake that is slow to clear out of my way.

Still, there was something that could fill me with terror. At night I was afraid of being attacked by the larger wild beasts, the lion and the leopard. I was stronger and better equipped than they, but I had had no personal experience of combat and I lacked the instincts that would have equipped me for the role of combatant. And even during the daytime I was afraid of big game hunters, particularly white men. Ah, those white men! They are the most dangerous of all the wild beasts. I was not afraid of their traps and snares and pits. Nor was it easy to drive me into an enclosure by trying to scare me with bonfires and clappers. As far as I was concerned, the menace was the camouflaged pit into which I might fall; so I was always very careful to examine the path ahead of me.

I could catch the wind of a village when several miles away from it, and I did my best to give all human habitations a very wide berth. I could even distinguish the different native tribes through my sense of smell. Some were a greater danger to me and others—less dangerous; some were no danger at all.

One day as I was feeling the wind with my outstretched trunk, I sensed a new smell; I could not decide whether it was from a wild beast or a man. Most likely from a man. I became inquisitive. After all, I was trying to learn everything I could about the forest. I had to know something about everything that was likely to be a danger to me. I followed the smell as one might follow a compass, moving very cautiously. It was during the night, at an hour when the natives are fast asleep. I continued on my way, while the scent grew stronger and stronger. I went as stealthily as possible, at the same time keeping a wary eye on the path ahead of me.

By morning I had reached the edge of a forest. I looked at the clearing before me, keeping myself concealed in the thick undergrowth. A pale moon hung over the forest, throwing an ashen light on a number of low, sharply-pointed huts. Huts of this kind could only give shelter to a man of medium height when crouched in a sitting position. All was quiet, not a dog was barking. I approached from the leeward side. I wondered who could be living in these tiny huts which seemed to have been built by children at play.

All at once a small creature resembling a man clambered through a hole in the ground. He rose to his feet and let out a low whistle. In response another creature leapt to the ground from the branch of a tree. Two more clambered out. They crowded round a larger hut about five feet high and went into some sort of conference. As the first rays of the sun shone from the sky I was able to see the pygmies—for this is the word for these strange creatures. I realized I had wandered into one of the villages of these smallest people in the world. Their skin was light brown, their hair almost red. Their bodies were shapely and well-proportioned, but they were not more than three to four feet tall. Some of these "children" had thick, curly beards. They conversed rapidly in high, squeaky voices.

It was a most interesting spectacle, yet I felt terrified. I would rather have encountered giants than these dwarfs who could strike such terror into me. In fact, I would rather have met a white man. Though they are so small, pygmies are the elephant's deadliest enemies. I knew this before I became an elephant. They are excellent archers and javelin-throwers,

They use poisoned arrows, a prick from one of which can kill an elephant. They creep up stealthily from behind, throw a net over the elephant's hind legs or plunge a sharp knife into the tendon of the Achilles, cutting it through. They scatter poisoned hooks and sticks round their villages.

Quickly I turned and began to run as fast as I had done when fleeing from the leopard. I heard shouts behind me and sounds of hot pursuit. If the path had been level I could easily have outdistanced them, but I had to avoid insurmountable obstacles as I hurried through the forest. And my pursuers were as nimble as monkeys, mobile as lizards, indefatigable as the Borzoi; they ran swiftly as though nothing was an obstacle to them. The pursuers drew closer and several javelins were hurled at me; but the dense vegetation served to protect me. By now I was panting and could have dropped to the ground out of weariness. Yet the little folk neither tripped nor stumbled, never for a moment fell back; they continued to pursue me.

I discovered by bitter experience that being an elephant was no easy matter; the entire life of an animal as huge and strong as the elephant consists of one constant struggle for existence which never abates for a single moment. I felt it was highly improbable that any elephant could really live to be 100 years old or more. With all the worries they have to contend with, they should surely die long before human beings do. But perhaps real elephants do not worry as I did. My human brain was too highly-strung, too easily agitated. I assure you that during those moments death itself seemed to me preferable to life with death always dogging me. Should I give up? Should I stand and face the poisoned javelins and arrows of my biped torturers? I was quite prepared to do just that; but my mood changed. To my great surprise my trunk picked up the strong smell of a herd of elephants. Could I, perhaps, find safety among the elephants?

The dense forest began to thin out and gradually merged into the savannah with its high, separated trees which still afforded me a chance of sheltering from the arrows of my pursuers.

I hurried forward zigzag fashion. Here it was not so easy for the pygmies as it had been in the forest. Although I was making a broad track, they were hampered by the strong stems of the savannah plants and grasses. The smell of elephants grew stronger, although I could not see them.

In my path I encountered deep pits with elephants captured in them; they looked like hens squatting in the sand. From time to time I saw heaps of dung. As I reached the first clump of trees I caught sight of a group of elephants sprawling on the ground. Others were standing by the trees, their trunks flourishing branches of trees like fans, their tails wagging to and fro. Their ears were raised high like sunshades. Others were bathing in a stream. I was running against the wind, so the elephants did not pick up my smell. Only when they heard my footsteps did the alarm go up. You would never imagine what occurred then! The elephants tramped about on the river bank trumpeting desperately. The lead elephant, instead of giving protection to the rear, was the first to turn tail, rushing into the water and swimming to the opposite bank. Cow elephants, anxious for their young, tried to defend them, although they were almost as large as the adult beasts. It was left to the cow elephants to protect the rear. Could my sudden appearance have so terrified them, or had they, in their frenzied flight, sensed some danger other than that which had caused me to take to flight?

With all my might I hurled myself into the water and crossed the river ahead of many of the cow elephants with their young; I tried to get ahead, so that the entire body of elephants would separate me from my pursuers. Of course, this was egoistic of me; but I noticed that, except for the cow elephants, all the others were behaving similarly. I heard the pygmies rush up to the river. Their squeaky voices mingled with the trumpeting of the elephants. Something tragic was occurring there, but I was too afraid to look back. I continued to run across the open ground. I never discovered how the river battle between the dwarf-people and giant-animals ended.

With the elephants I ran for several hours. I was so tired that I could scarcely keep up with them. But I was determined not to be left behind. If the elephants would include me in their company I would be in comparative safety; they knew the locality and they knew their enemies better than I did.

XI. With the Elephant Herd

At long last the lead elephant halted and the others did the same. We all turned and looked about us. The pursuit was over. Only two young elephants and one cow were running after us!

It seemed as though my presence was being ignored until the last of the stragglers caught up with us and the elephants had quietened down a little. Then one or two of them came up and sniffed at me with their trunks; they looked me over or merely walked round me. They made soft, muttering noises, apparently asking me something; but I could not reply. I didn't even understand the meaning of the sounds they made, whether they were of disapproval or of satisfaction.

Most of all I feared the lead elephant. I knew I had been a lead elephant before Wagner operated on me. Suppose this was the same herd; suppose the new lead elephant were to begin disputing with me for power? I confess I became very nervous when the huge, strong lead elephant came close and, as though by accident, its tusk prodded my side. But I remained submissive. A second time he prodded me, as though challenging me to combat. But I refused the challenge and merely moved aside. Then the elephant rolled up its trunk and, holding it lightly between the lips, stuffed it into its mouth. Later I learned that this is the elephant's way of expressing dismay or surprise. The lead elephant was evidently puzzled at my submissiveness; he was at a loss to know how to behave. At the same time I had not learned the language of elephants, so thinking this was its way of welcoming me, I also stuffed my trunk into my mouth. The elephant squealed and moved away.

I understand every elephant sound now. I know that the soft, rumbling sort of sound and the squealing sound both signify satisfaction. Terror is expressed by a loud, roaring sound; sudden fright by a short, sharp sound. When I first made my appearance, the herd had responded with just such short, sharp sounds. When in a frenzy, because injured or being tormented, they make deep, glottal sounds. One of the elephants left by the river bank made this sound when the pygmies attacked. Perhaps a poisoned arrow had mortally wounded him. When elephants attack an enemy, they let out a penetrating, screeching sound. I am giving here only the basic "words" of the elephant vocabulary, those which express the more important sensations. But there are shades of meaning to these "words."

At first I very much feared the elephants would guess that I was no ordinary elephant and that they would chase me out of the herd. Perhaps they did sense that something was wrong about me, but, as it turned out, they felt peacefully disposed towards me. They treated me rather like a defective juvenile who is not quite right in the head, but who would not harm anyone.

My existence was now pretty monotonous. Everywhere we went in single file. Between ten and eleven in the morning we rested until three in the afternoon; then we began to pasture again. During the night we rested for a few hours as well. Some of the elephants lay down, almost all of them dozed, but one kept watch.

Somehow I could not reconcile myself to the idea of spending the rest of my life with a herd of elephants. I longed for human beings. I may have the appearance of an elephant, but I prefer living peacefully and carefree with ordinary people. I would readily have gone to the white people, but I was afraid they would kill me for my tusks. I confess I tried hard to damage my tusks and so become valueless in the eyes of human beings, but nothing came of it. Either the tusks are unbreakable or I did not know how to go about the business. And so I roamed about with the elephants for more than a month.

One day we were pasturing in the open with the boundless savannah all round us. I was on guard. It was a starry night; there was no moon. All was relatively still in the herd. I moved some distance away, the better to listen and pick up the scent of the nocturnal smells. But all I could smell were the various grasses, the smaller reptiles, the harmless animals. Suddenly a light flared up some distance away, almost on the horizon. It went out, then again flared up and burst into flames.

A few moments passed and then, to the left of the first blaze, another light shone out, then a third and fourth some distance farther away. These were not big game hunters camping for the night. The fires were burning at regular distances forming, as it were, a row of lamps switched on along a highway. Then, at the same moment, I noticed similar flickering lights from fires on the other side. We were between two lines of fires. Soon at one end of this high road between the two rows of fires, hunters would begin firing and shouting, while at the other end either pits or enclosures awaited us. It all depended on whether the hunters wanted to catch us alive or dead. If we fell into the pits, we would break a leg and be good for nothing but slaughter; in the enclosures, a life of slavery awaited us. Elephants are afraid of fire. In general, when noise awakens them, they show cowardice and rush off in the direction away from the fires and noise; but there the silent trap or death awaits them.

I alone of the whole herd understood the situation. But was this an advantage? What should I do? Should I go towards the fires? There I would meet armed men. I might have the good fortune to break through the blockade, but then I would have to be separated from the herd and begin life as a hermit elephant. Sooner or later a bullet, a poisoned arrow or the fangs of some wild beast would kill me.

I still seemed to be hesitating, yet actually my choice had already been made for, without realising it, I had withdrawn a little from the others, in order that when the awakened herd stampeded, I would not be drawn into catastrophe in the whirlpool of elephant bodies.

By now the hunters were shouting, beating drums, flourishing rattles, whistling and firing. I let out a deep, trumpeting call. The elephants woke up and trampled about in terror, trumpeting their loudest. The extraordinary din seemed to rock the ground. The animals looked about them and saw the fires apparently creeping closer and closer. Actually they were being carried nearer and nearer. The elephants ceased their trumpeting and rushed off in one direction, but the sound of the hunters grew louder and they made off in the opposite direction ... to destruction. True, death was not yet so very near. The hunt continues for several days. The fires would continue to close in, the hunters would come closer and closer and drive the elephants slowly forward until finally they would find themselves in the pits or the enclosures.

But I did not go with the elephants; I remained alone. The panicky terror which had seized the entire herd had been transmitted to my elephant nerves and from them to my human brain. Fear almost overshadowed my conscious mind; I was almost ready to rush after the herd, but I summoned all my human courage, all my will power, to my aid. No! My human brain must master my elephant fear, must conquer the huge mountain of flesh, blood and bones that was trying to draw me to destruction.

Acting like a lorry-driver, I turned the "wheel" of my "lorry" and made straight for the river. A splash, a cascade of spray, stillness. The water cooled my burning elephant blood. Reason had won. Now my elephant feet were held fast in the "reins" of reason. They were tramping obediently about on the silty bed of the river.

I decided to submerge myself completely in the water like a hippopotamus—something no ordinary elephant would ever think of doing. I would breathe through the tip of my trunk. At least, I did try to, but the water felt uncomfortable in my eyes and ears. From time to time I raised my head to listen. The hunters had drawn closer. I submerged again. Finally the hunters made off without noticing me.

By now I had had as much as I could stand of these constant fears and agitations. Whatever else happened, I would not give myself up to big game hunters. I would swim down the Congo in search of some factory. There were several between Stanleypool and Bom. I would turn up at some farm or factory and do my best to show the people that I was not a wild elephant. I would show them that I was trained. They would not kill me or drive me away.

XII. In the Service of Ivory-Poachers

I found that this plan was more difficult to carry out than I had imagined. I soon found myself in the main stream of the Congo, swimming with the current. During the daylight hours I swam close to the bank, but at night I kept to the current. My journey was safe enough. This part of the river is navigable, but savage tribes are afraid to approach the banks. In the course of my entire journey down the river—and it continued for about a month—I only once heard the roar of a lion and, on one occasion, I had a rather unpleasant encounter, or rather a collision, with a hippopotamus. It was at night. It was wallowing in the river with only its nostrils above water. I had not noticed it, but I knocked against the clumsy creature while I was swimming, like a ship encountering an iceberg. The animal went completely under water, its blunt muzzle began buffeting me painfully in the stomach. I hurriedly swam away from it, while the hippo came to the surface, snorted angrily and swam after me. Still, I managed to get myself clear of it. I swam on until I safely reached Lukungi, where there stood a large Belgian factory; or so I imagined it to be judging by the flag it was flying.

Early in the morning I left the forest and walked towards a house, nodding my head. But this did not help me. Two enormous watchdogs barked ferociously and set upon me. A man in a white shirt emerged from the house, but hurried indoors again at the sight of me. Several Negroes came shouting across the yard and took shelter in the house. And then ... two rifle shots rang out. I did not wait for the third. I was compelled to abandon the place and return to the forest.

One night I was ambling through a sparse and dreary forest, of which there are several in Central Africa. The vegetation was dark, the ground underfoot swampy, the tree trunks black. Heavy rain had recently fallen and the night was fairly cool for the Equator, and a light breeze was blowing. Like other elephants I am a little sensitive to the damp, in spite of my thick skin. When it rains or the atmosphere is damp, I always keep on the move to keep warm.

I had been going at a steady pace for several hours when I caught sight of a campfire. I was in a pretty wild part; not a single Negro village was to be seen. Who could have built the fire? I went a little faster. The forest came to an end and before me was the low grassland of the savannah. There must recently have been a forest fire and the grass had not yet grown to its natural height. An old, dilapidated hut stood about half a mile from the forest; beside it a campfire was burning and near it two men, evidently Europeans. One of them was stirring food in a cauldron slung over the fire. A third, handsome fellow—obviously a native and half-naked—stood like a bronze statue not far from the fire.

Slowly, with my eyes fixed on the men, I went towards the fire. When they saw me I dropped to my knees like a trained elephant presenting its back for a load. The smaller man in a sun-helmet grabbed a rifle, clearly intending to shoot. But at the same moment the native cried out in broken English.

"Don't shoot it! It's a good, trained elephant!" He ran towards me.

"Get away or I'll make a hole in you! Hi, you, what's your name?" cried the white man, taking aim.

"M-pepo," replied the native without moving away. He stood closer to me as though to put his body between me and the bullet.

"Can't you see it's a tame, bana,"* he said, stroking my trunk.

---

* Gentleman

"Get away, you ape!" shouted the man with the rifle. "I'm going to shoot it! One, two. . . ."

"Hold your fire, Bakala," said the other white man, who was tall and lean. "Mpepo's right. We've collected enough tusks and it won't be cheap or easy to carry them even as far as Mathadi. Sure, the elephant's tame. We won't ask about its master and how it comes to be prowling about at night. We can make good use of it. An elephant can lift a ton, though it wouldn't get far with such a load. Let's say, half a ton. After all, an elephant can do the work of thirty or forty bearers. You see, it won't cost us a penny. And when we don't need it any more, we can kill it, and we'll add its fine tusks to our collection, see?"

Bakala listened impatiently, making several attempts to take aim. But as his companion calculated what it would cost to hire bearers instead of using the elephant, he was finally persuaded and put down the rifle.

"Hi, you, what's your name!" he yelled to the native.

"M-pepo," came the ready reply. Later I learned that Bakala always used the same words to address the native, and the latter invariably replied in the same way, emphasizing the "M", as though he found some difficulty in pronouncing his own name.

"Come here. Lead the elephant."

I willingly obeyed Mpepo's sign inviting me to come closer to the fire.

"What shall we call him, eh? Truant suits him, don't you think, Cox?"

I looked at Cox. His predominant colour was blue. His nose was particularly striking; it looked as though it had just emerged from a pot of blue paint. On his bluish body he wore a blue shirt, open at the neck, sleeves rolled to the elbow. He had a hoarse voice and a burring, lisping way of talking which also seemed blue to me. The hoarse voice seemed faded, like the shirt.

"All right," he agreed. "Let him be Truant."

There was a movement from a bundle of rags close to the fire and a low bass voice asked:

"What's going on?"

"So you're still alive, and I thought you'd died," said Bakala coolly to the bundle of rags.

The bundle shifted again and a large arm flung aside the rags. A big, well-proportioned man sat up, propped on his arms, his body swaying a little. His face was very pale, the reddish beard rumpled. The man was evidently very ill, his face was pale as death. The dull eyes regarded me, and he smiled.

"A fourth has joined the three tramps," he remarked. "White skin—black soul. Black skin—white soul. Only one honest man, and that a bakuba!" He fell back, helpless.

"He's delirious," remarked Bakala.

"His delirium is somehow insulting," replied Cox. "He's talking in riddles: one honest man, and that a bakuba. You know what he means. Mpepo's from the Bakuba tribe. You've only to look at his teeth for proof: the upper incisors have been knocked out. That's the Bakuba custom. So he's the only honest one, we're all scoundrels."

"Including Brown. His skin's whiter than ours, so his soul's blacker. Brown, you're a scoundrel too."

But Brown did not reply.

"He's unconscious again."

"So much the better, and better still if he dies. He's not much use to us now; he's only a hindrance."

"But if he recovers, he'll be worth two of us."

"That's a lot of satisfaction! Why can't you understand he's just one too many?"

Brown muttered something in his delirium, and the conversation came to an end.

"Hi, you, what's your name?"

"M-pepo . . . ."

"Hobble the elephant and tie it to a tree, so he doesn't get away."

"No, he won't go away," replied Mpepo, stroking my leg.

The next morning I took a closer look at my new masters. Best of all I liked Mpepo. He was always cheerful and smiling, his white teeth, a little disfigured because of the absence of two upper incisors, gleaming white. Mpepo evidently liked elephants and he took good care of me. He washed my ears, eyes and legs and the heavy folds of skin. He brought me gifts—delicious fruits and berries which he searched out specially for me.

Brown was still a sick man, and I could get no real impression of what he was like. His face attracted me and also his direct manner of talking to his companions. But I felt a decided dislike of Bakala and Cox. Bakala in particular made a very strange and unpleasant impression, in his dirty, ragged suit. It was well-cut and of the finest material and may have belonged to an extremely wealthy traveller. I felt that Bakala had acquired both the suit and the tent by underhand means. Perhaps he had robbed and then murdered some famous British explorer. The magnificent rifle could also have belonged to an Englishman. And he carried a large revolver and a knife of terrifying proportions in his broad belt. He was Portuguese or Spanish, a sort of outlaw with no country, no family, no definite occupation.

Cox, with his faded blue appearance, was certainly an Englishman who had evidently come up against the laws of his country. All three were ivory-poachers, hunting elephants purely for their tusks, with no regard at all for laws or frontiers.

Mpepo acted as their guide and instructor. Although he was so young, he was an expert on elephants and elephant-tracking. True, his methods were rough and savage, but he knew of no others. He used the methods he had learned from his ancestors. As for the other men, it was all the same to them how the elephants were killed. They caught them half-suffocated and scorched in a ring of fires, they caught them in pits with sharp staves at the bottom, they shot them out of hand, they cut through the veins of the hind legs, they stunned them with logs dropped from trees. They simply finished them off. Mpepo was most useful to them.

XIII. Truant Plays a Prank

One day when Brown, though better, was still too weak to go hunting elephants, Cox and Bakala mounted my back and we set off to a place several miles distant to collect the tusks of an elephant killed the previous day. The men were conversing freely, for they thought they could not be overheard; to them I was just a draught animal.

"The chocolate-coloured ape—what do they call him—will have to be paid one-fifth; that was the agreement," Bakala was saying.

"It'll be profitable enough," replied Cox.

"Then we'll have to divide what's left into three: you, me and Brown. Reckoned at 40 to 50 marks a pound of ivory. . . ."

"There's not a chance of getting that much. You've no head for business. There's what is known as soft or dead ivory and hard or live ivory. The first is only called soft; actually it is very hard and white and fine, the sort used for billiard balls, piano keys and combs, and it's valued at a high price. But the elephants here don't give that sort of ivory. You have to go to East Africa to get it. Only there, they'll make soft bones of your hard ones before they'll ever let you kill a single elephant. Hereabouts elephant ivory is hard, living, transparent. It can only be used for the handles of umbrellas and walking-sticks, and for the cheaper combs.

"Then what's the great idea?" Bakala asked. "What are we working for?"

"Not for nothing. Someone will profit from it. If four of us hunt and we divide our gains in half, then it won't be all that bad!"

"I'd already got that idea myself."

"It's not your place to think, you just have to act. Brown will be on his legs in a day or two and then it'll be too late to settle accounts with him. The red devil's as strong as an ox. And Mpepo's as agile as a monkey. We've got to get rid of them with one fell swoop. Best of all at night. And get them drunk first, just to be on the safe side. We've still got enough drink for them."

"When?"

"Ah, here we are...."

The unfortunate elephant lay on its side in the deep pit, its belly slit open by a sharp stave three days previously. It was still alive. Bakala shot it dead, climbed into the pit with Cox and began to hack out the tusks. The work took them almost the whole day. The sun was already sinking in the west when they roped the tusks to my back and we began the return journey.

The camp was already in sight when Cox returned to their interrupted conversation.

"There's no need to postpone it," he said. "Let's make it tonight."

But they were to be disappointed. They were surprised to find that Brown was not at the camp. Mpepo explained that the "bana" had felt well enough to go hunting and would probably not return that night. Bakala swore under his breath. So the murder had to be put off to some other time.

Early next morning while Cox and Bakala were still asleep Brown returned. He went up to Mpepo and touched him lightly on the shoulder. The native, who was keeping watch, smiled broadly, his teeth gleaming. Brown beckoned him aside, led him up to me and ordered him to mount. At a sign from Mpepo I knelt down and they both mounted; I carried them along by the edge of the forest.

"I want to take them a present. They think I'm ill, but I'm all right. During the night I killed an enormous elephant with magnificent tusks. It will be a surprise for Bakala and Cox."

By the light of the rising sun I saw the enormous swollen elephant carcase lying on its side in a thicket of coffee bushes by the river bank.

When the work on the tusks was finished, we set off for the camp—to meet our doom. Brown and Mpepo would soon encounter death, and I was to share their fate at a later date. Of course, I could always escape from the men. But as no immediate danger threatened me and I wanted, if I could, to save Brown and Mpepo, I made no attempt to get away. I was particularly sorry for Mpepo; he was such a happy, carefree youth, with the body of an Apollo. But how could I warn them? I couldn't tell them of the danger they faced ... but I could refuse to carry them to the camp, perhaps?

Immediately I turned sharply off the path and headed for the Congo river. I thought that once we had reached the river we might meet some human beings, and Brown would be able to return to some civilized country. But he did not understand why I was so stubborn and he began to strike me on the neck with a pointed iron bar. The point pricked my skin which is very sensitive and turns septic easily. I remembered how long it had taken for the wound from the Englishman's bullet to heal, after he had fired at me from the boat. I heard Mpepo pleading with Brown not to pierce the skin on my neck; but the man was so infuriated because of my disobedience that he only prodded harder and deeper.

In an effort to persuade me, Mpepo spoke comforting words to me in his own language, though I couldn't understand a word of it. But the tone of voice is understood equally by man and beast; that much I could understand. He leaned over and kissed my neck. Poor Mpepo! If only he could have known what he was asking me to do!

"Kill him and put an end to it!" yelled Brown. "If Truant doesn't want to fetch and carry, then he's not wanted, except for his tusks. The pampered beast! Truant, indeed! It's more than likely he abandoned his owners, and now he wants to escape from us. But he won't! I'll put a bullet between his eye and ear first!"

The words sent a shudder through me. Brown, the elephant hunter, could hardly miss if he fired from the back of an elephant. Should I let myself be killed or should I carry them to certain death? I could hear Mpepo imploring Brown to spare me. But the Englishman was adamant; he had already taken the rifle from his shoulder.

Before it was too late I suddenly turned towards the camp.

"You'd think the beast understood the language and knew what I was going to do," said Brown, laughing.

Submissively I walked a few steps then swiftly seized Brown in my trunk, swung him round and hurled him to the ground. Then I hurried off into the forest carrying Mpepo on my back. Brown shouted and cursed. He was not really hurt, but being still weak from his illness, he had been unable to pick himself up quickly enough. I had taken advantage of this and had reached the forest.

"If I can't save both of them," I thought, "at least I'll save Mpepo."

But the native, too, wanted to keep with the campers. It was not for nothing that he had been risking his life for several months hunting elephants. He was due to be paid. I should have pinned Mpepo down with my trunk, but the idea had not occurred to me, for I felt sure he would hesitate before jumping from the height of my back. But the lad was as agile as a monkey and so he behaved differently; as I was passing close to the forest, he grabbed a branch and leapt on to a bough. Mpepo was now out of my reach, so I stood still under the tree, waiting... until I sensed Brown creeping up stealthily behind me. Then I made a dash for the thicket before he could fire at me.

At last they were gone. Yet I didn't want to leave them to their fate. After waiting a while, I went back to the path, made a detour and reached the camp before them. Cox and Bakala were most surprised to see me without any riders, but with good tusks on my back.

"Can the elephants and wild beasts have aided us in getting rid of Brown and Mpepo?" asked Cox, as he untied the ropes.

But their pleasure was premature. Soon Brown arrived, cursing; Mpepo was with him. When Brown saw me he let out a fresh torrent of oaths. He related the story of how I had played a prank on them; he tried to get them to kill me outright. Cox, calculating as usual, was against the idea and simply went on with his job. He and Bakala said how pleased he was that Brown was well again and that he had returned safely to the camp, particularly with such a magnificent pair of tusks.

They all turned in early. Mpepo slept like an infant. Brown, quite worn out, slept soundly too. Cox was keeping watch and Bakala was tossing under his blanket, evidently wakeful. Several times Bakala raised his head and looked enquiringly at Cox, who shook his head to denote it was not yet time.

The waning moon appeared beyond the forest, shedding a dim light over the clearing. There was a pitiful cry, like that of an infant; somewhere in the forest a small creature was probably caught and held in the teeth of a wild beast. The sound did not rouse Brown who was evidently still sleeping soundly. Cox gave a nod and Bakala, who had been watching his every movement, rose at once, his hand feeling behind him for the revolver in his back pocket. I decided it was time for me, too, to act. I did what Indian elephants do in order to scare the enemy: I pressed the tip of my trunk to the ground and blew hard. The result was a strange, frightening noise, something between a crackling and gurgling and snuffling and loud enough to wake the dead; and Brown was by no means dead.

"Who the devil's playing the trombone?" he asked, raising his head, his sleepy eyes goggling. Quickly Bakala squatted on the ground.

"What d'you think you're doing, dancing a jig?" asked Brown.

"I . . . er . . . the cursed elephant woke me up. Get out, you!"

But I didn't get out, and some time later, when Brown was again sleeping soundly, I repeated the performance. Cox was already close to Brown, his revolver ready, when I trumpeted with all my might. Brown leapt up, rushed at me and hit the end of my trunk with his open palm. Quickly I furled my trunk and moved aside.

"I'll murder it, curse the brute!" he yelled. "It's not an elephant, it's a devil. Mpepo! Drive the beast away to a swamp.... And what're you doing with a revolver?" he asked suddenly, looking suspiciously at Cox.

"I was just going to send a couple of bullets after Truant to help him farther on his way."

Brown again settled on the ground and was dozing again. I stood only a few paces away, watching the camp.

"Blast the elephant!" hissed Cox, shaking his fist at me.

"He's caught the wind of a wild beast," said Mpepo. The lad was trying to justify me; he little suspected how near he was to the truth. I had certainly trumpeted because I had caught the wind of wild beasts—merciless, two-legged beasts.

It was almost morning when Cox finally nodded to Bakala. Swiftly they ran forward: Cox towards Brown, Bakala towards Mpepo, firing simultaneously. Mpepo let out a pitiful, penetrating wail like the tiny creature that had cried out earlier in the night. Then he stood up, shook himself and fell to the ground, his legs working spasmodically. Brown made no sound. It all happened so quickly that there had been no time for me to warn the unfortunate creatures....

But Brown was still alive. Suddenly he lifted himself on the right elbow and shot Cox, who was just bending over him. Cox was felled to the ground. Brown took cover behind his body and fired at Bakala.

"Ah, you red-headed cheat!" cried Bakala. Once he fired back and then took to his heels. But he had only gone a few paces when he twirled round on the spot and fell to the ground. A bullet had hit him in the head. Brown heaved a sigh and dropped prone on the ground. An unpleasant smell of blood filled the air in the clearing. All was absolutely still,

except for Brown's wheezing. I went closer and looked into
his face; the eyes were already glassy. He made a convulsive
movement and fired again. The bullet slightly grazed the skin
on the knee of my right foreleg.

XV. A Successful Manoeuvre

I had my first good fortune when I finally arrived at
Mathadi. It was one evening when the sun was just setting
behind the mountain peaks separating the Congo basin from
the sea. I was in the forest not far from the river, my mind
full of sad thoughts. I was beginning to regret I had not run
with the herd into the enclosure. Then I would not now be
wandering about like an exile: either all my earthly suffer-
ings would have been at an end or I would have become an
honest, working elephant. To the right of me, through the
thicket of forest along the river bank, the river glowed ruby-
red in the rays of the setting sun. To the left were gigantic
rubber trees with cuts in the bark, which indicated that there
must be people not far away.

Another hundred yards or so and I came out into cultivat-
ed fields of manioc, millet, bananas, pineapples, sugar cane
and tobacco. Carefully I followed the path between the sugar canes and tobacco plants until it brought me to an open
field, where a house stood in the middle. No one was to be
seen near the house, but not far away were two children
playing hoop-la, a boy and a girl, seven or eight years old.

They did not notice me as I went into the field. I rose
to my hind legs, made a squeaky noise as funnily as I knew
how to and danced about. When they caught sight of me
the children stood amazed. I was so overjoyed that they
did not cry or run away that I began to caper about and
perform in a way no properly trained elephant would have

dreamed of doing. The boy was the first to show his pleasure by bursting into fits of laughter, while the little girl clapped her hands. I went on dancing and gamboling about, standing first on my forelegs, then on my hind legs and curvetting around.

Growing bolder the children came closer, until finally I stretched out my trunk, inviting the boy to take a swing on it. After some hesitation he sat himself on the end of my curved trunk and swung on it. Then I gave the little girl a swing, too. I must say I was so glad of the company of these carefree little white children that I became quite engrossed in playing with them; I did not notice a tall, lean man approaching. His complexion was yellowish, his eyes hollow; he had evidently only recently recovered from an attack of tropical fever. He stood and watched dumbfounded and indescribably astounded.

"Papa, Papa!" cried the boy. "See what a hoity-toity we've got!"

"Hoity-Toity!" echoed the father, hoarsely. He continued to stand quite still, his arms hanging loosely at his sides; he had no idea what to do. I made elephant bows to him, I even dropped on my knees. The man shook me by the trunk and smiled.

"Ah! Victory at last!" I thought, rejoicing.

* * *

And here the elephant's story ends. His entire history could really end here; what ultimately happened to him is of no particular interest. However, Wagner, Denisov and the elephant went on an excellent tour of Switzerland. Much to the surprise of the tourists, the elephant strolled about the outskirts of Vevey, which in earlier days Ring had loved to visit. Sometimes the animal bathed in the Lac de Genève, but the cold weather arrived rather early that year, unfortunately, driving our tourists back to Berlin by special goods van.

Hoity-Toity is still performing at the Busch Circus, earning an honest eight hundred pound ration and astounding not only Berliners but the numerous foreigners who make special journeys to Berlin to see the "elephant genius." Scientists are still arguing about why he is such a genius. Some say it's all a "trick," some call it "conditioned reflex," others refer to it as "mass hypnosis."

Jung is now extremely polite and solicitous and takes great care of the elephant. Deep down, Jung is really afraid of Hoity-Toity, regarding the whole thing as the work of the devil. But you may judge for yourselves: every day the elephant peruses the newspapers, and once he pilfered a box of patience cards out of Jung's pocket. And, what do you think? When Jung took a look at the elephant one day, he found him laying out the cards and playing patience on a large, upturned barrel. Jung kept this to himself; he has no wish to be considered a liar!

* * *

Written from the documents of Akim Ivanovich Denisov. After reading the manuscript, I. S. Wagner added the following words:

"All this actually did happen. You are requested not to translate this material into German. Ring's secret must at least be kept a secret from the people closely in touch with him."

ARKADY STRUGATSKY, BORIS STRUGATSKY

SPONTANEOUS REFLEX

1

Urm was bored.

Actually only man and a few animals are capable of boredom as a reaction to a monotonous situation or inner dissatisfaction with oneself, when one loses interest in life. To be bored, there must be something that gets bored—a delicate, perfectly organized nervous system. One has to know how to think or, at any rate, to suffer. Urm had no nervous system in the ordinary sense of the word, and he could not think, still less suffer. He could only perceive, remember and act. And yet he was bored.

Roughly speaking, it was all because after the Master went out there was nothing new left for him to remember. And yet, to accumulate recollections had become the purpose of Urm's existence. He was possessed by an insatiable curiosity, an insatiable longing to perceive and remember as much as possible. Every fact and phenomenon in space and time which could be a source of sensation for any one of his fifteen sense organs was good enough for the purpose. If there were no unknown facts and phenomena, they had to be looked for.

Meanwhile the state of affairs round Urm was familiar to him down to the last feature, the last shade. The spacious square room with grey, rather rough walls, the low ceiling and iron door were things he remembered from the first moment of his existence. Here there was always a smell of hot metal and greased insulation. Somewhere overhead there was a low, muffled humming; people could not hear it without special instruments, but Urm could hear it perfectly. The daylight lamps under the ceiling were extinguished, but Urm could see the room perfectly well by infra-red light and by the vibrations reaching his locators.

And so Urm was bored, and he decided to set out in search of new impressions. Half an hour had passed since the Master had left and he knew by experience that the Master would not return very soon. This was very important, because Urm had once taken a walk round the room without the order being given, and when the Master found him occupied in this way he fixed things so that Urm was able to be tortured with curiosity but was unable to move even a locator horn. There was evidently no fear of this now.

Urm staggered and moved heavily forward. The cement floor echoed under his heavy rubber soles and Urm stopped for a moment to listen; he even bent down. But there was nothing unfamiliar in the gamut of sounds emanating from the vibrating cement, and Urm hurried again towards the opposite wall. He went right up to it and sniffed. The wall smelt of damp concrete and rusty iron. Nothing new. Then Urm turned round, scratching the wall with his sharp steel elbow, crossed the room diagonally and stopped in front of the door. It was not so easy to open the door and for a time Urm examined the lock, comparing what he saw with what he already knew. Finally he stretched out the toothed claw of his left hand, skilfully grasped the small lever of the lock and turned it. The door opened with a feeble, prolonged creak. That was something interesting at last, and Urm spent several minutes opening and shutting the door, at first quickly, then slowly, listening and remembering. Then he stepped over the threshold and found a staircase in front of him. It was a narrow one, with stone steps, and it was fairly high—in a moment Urm had counted eighteen steps up to the first landing, where a light was burning. Urm knew what steps were and began to mount them leisurely. From the landing another staircase, a wooden one, went up higher; it had ten steps. To the right was a broad passage. After hesitating for a moment, Urm turned to the right. He did not know why he did so. The passage was no more interesting than the staircase. True, the staircase was considerably narrower.

Warm air came from the corridor and it was brightly lit by infra-red light. This light was radiated by ribbed cylinders standing low over the floor. Urm had never before seen the radiators of steam central heating. At any rate, the ribbed cylinders interested him. He bent down and clapped both claws round one of them. There was a sharp metallic crack and a grinding sound; a thick cloud of hot steam, shining like a scrap of the sun, rose to the ceiling. A jet of boiling water gushed round Urm's feet. He raised the cylinder to his head and examined it closely; then he extended the flexible feelers of his micromanipulators from his breastplate and carefully investigated the torn edge of the tube. Then the feelers were tucked away again, the cylinder fell to the floor and Urm's rubber soles splashed through the puddles. He went as far as the end of the passage. Over a low door there, a red inscription shone out: "Caution! No entrance without special clothing!" read Urm. He knew the word "caution," but he also knew that the word always referred to people. The word could not refer to him, Urm. He put out a hand and pushed the door.

Yes, here there was much that was interesting and new. He stood at the entrance to a spacious hall, filled with metal, stone and plastic objects. In the centre of the hall was a metre high concrete erection, resembling a flat pedestal covered with an iron or lead shield. Numerous cables ran from it to the walls along which stretched marble tiles with shining instruments and the switch handles of electric switches. The concrete pedestal was surrounded by a fence of copper wire, and shining elbow-like sticks hung from the ceiling. The sticks ended in pincers and claws like those on Urm's arms.

Moving softly over the tiled floor, Urm approached the copper wire fence, walked round it and then stood still. Then he walked round it a second time. He could find no way through the wire netting. So he raised his foot and walked through it without effort. Ragged pieces of copper netting hung from his shoulders. But before he had taken two steps towards the concrete pedestal he stopped short. His head, round as a schoolroom globe, turned watchfully from side to side, the ebonite shells of his acoustic receptors were thrust out and waved about, the locator horns quivered. The leaden lid of the pedestal was radiating infra-red light, noticeable even in this heated hall. But in addition some sort of ultra-violet radiation was coming from it. Urm could see very well in X-rays and gamma-rays and it seemed to him that the lid was transparent and that beneath it lay a narrow, bottomless well full of shining dust. In the depths of his memory swam the command: leave this place at once! Urm did not know when the order had been given or by whom. Probably, he already knew it when he came into existence, just as he knew much more than he had ever seen or experienced. But Urm did not obey the order. Curiosity got the better of him. He bent over the pedestal, extended his claw-like hands and with something of an effort raised the lid.

A flood of gamma-rays blinded him. Red lights winked alarmingly on marble control panels, a siren howled. For a moment, through the transparent silhouettes of his hands he saw the inside of the concrete pit, then he threw down the lid and pronouced in a low, husky voice:

"Opasnost! Gefahr! Danger! Wei hsien! Abunai!"

A deep echo rolled round the hall and died away. Urm turned the upper part of his body 180° and hurriedly moved to the exit. The shock caused by the flood of radioactive particles in the control counters drove him from the concrete pedestal. Of course, the cruellest rays, the most powerful flood of particles could not cause Urm the slightest harm; even being in the active zone of the reactor could not have serious consequences for him. But, in constructing Urm, the Master had put in him a desire to keep as far away as possible from sources of intense radiation.

Urm went out into the corridor and carefully shut the door behind him. Stepping over the ribbed cylinder of the steam heating system, he found himself once more on the staircase landing. There he immediately caught sight of someone hurriedly descending the wooden staircase.

It was someone much shorter than the Master, someone wearing loose-fitting, light-coloured clothing, who had unusually long hair, the colour of gold. Urm had never seen people like this before. He sniffed at the air and experienced the familiar scent of white lilac. Sometimes the Master smelt the same way, but only faintly so.

The landing was in semi-darkness, the staircase behind the girl was brightly lit, and the girl did not immediately notice the clumsy outlines of Urm's enormous figure. But, hearing his footsteps, she stopped and cried out angrily:

"Who's there? Is that you, Ivashev?"

"*Zdravstvuite, kak pozhivaete?*"* lisped Urm.

The girl shrieked. Moving towards her out of the gloom she

---

* "Good day, how do you do?"

saw a shining head with narrow, glassy eyes, excessively broad, armour-plated shoulders, and thick jointed arms. Urm advanced to the bottom step of the wooden staircase and the girl shrieked again.

Never before had Man refused to respond to Urm's greeting, yet this strange, high-pitched sund, sharp and penetrating, and most certainly incoherent did not correspond to any of the replies which Urm knew. Urm's interest was aroused and he moved resolutely after the fleeing girl. The wooden steps groaned and creaked under his feet.

"Back!" shrieked the girl.

Urm stopped, then bent his head to listen.

"Back, you monster!"

Urm knew the command "back!" It meant that he must turn the upper part of his body in a circle and take a few steps in the opposite direction until another command was given "Stop!" But it was usually the Master who gave the orders, still more Urm wanted to investigate. He began climbing again until he found himself at the door of a small, lighted room.

"Back! Back! Back!" yelled the girl.

This time Urm did not stop although he did move more slowly than he might have done. The room interested him: two writing-desks, chairs, a draughtsman's board, a bookcase and thick files. While Urm was busily moving boxes, untying files and reading aloud the inscriptions written clearly in black Indian ink on the edges of the blue prints, the girl slipped away to the next room, took cover behind a divan and seized the telephone receiver. Urm saw this because he had an optical receiver at the back of his neck, but the little long-haired person did not interest him any more. Stepping over the papers scattered on the floor, he proceeded further. Behind him the girl was shouting into the telephone:

"Is that Nikolai Petrovich? This is Galya! Nikolai Petrovich, your Urm has broken in on us! Urm! Uliana-Robert-Mama. . . . Yes! I don't know. . . . I met him coming out of the big reactor hall. . . . Yes, yes, he had been in the reactor room. . . . What? Evidently not."

Urm stopped listening. He went out into the foyer and stood there, rooted to the spot, rapidly moving the black horns of his locators. He was astounded. On the opposite wall hung something large, shining and cold. In infra-red light it seemed like a grey, impenetrable rectangle and it shone and turned silver in ordinary rays, but this was not the object that dismayed Urm. In the strange rectangle stood a black monster with a head that was as round as a schoolroom globe and surmounted by quivering horns. Urm could not understand where it was. His visual distance-meter informed him that twelve metres and eight centimetres separated him from the unfamiliar object, yet the locator contradicted this. "There is no object at all. There is only a smooth, almost vertical surface at a distance of six metres and eight centimetres." Never before had Urm seen anything of the kind, and never had the locator and the visual receiver given him such contradictory information. From the outset something had been inserted in his organism that demanded that he make clear and comprehensible everything he might have to touch, so he moved resolutely forward, incidentally noting and storing in his memory the governing rule in this case: "the distance according to the visual distance-meter is twice the distance according to the locator. . . ." He walked into the mirror. The glass broke into a tinkling shower of splinters and Urm, pressed against the wall, stopped. Evidently there was nothing more to do here. He scratched the plaster, sniffed, then turned and walked to the exit, ignoring the man on duty who, with a face as white as a sheet, was pulling at the alarm signal Outside a snow-storm was raging and he found himself enveloped in white darkness.

2

When Nikolai Petrovich put down the receiver, Piskunov was already in the front hall hurriedly getting into his fur coat.

"Where are you off to?"

"I'm going over, of course. . . ."

"Wait, we've got to decide on a plan of action. If that cumbersome mechanism starts frisking about in the power-station. . . ."

"It's not so bad if it's only the power-station," retorted Ryabkin. "But what about the laboratory? And the stores? And what if he looks in here, the settlement?"

Nikolai Petrovich thought hard. Impatiently Piskunov stood shifting from one foot to the other, his hand on the door handle.

"We've got to hurry over there, all of us," Kostenko timidly suggested. "We must find him and . . . er . . . grab him."

Piskunov merely frowned; Ryabkin muttered angrily to himself as he fumbled at the clothes hooks to find his fur coat.

"A nice thing to say, grab him! And how would you suggest we do it? By the slack of his trousers? He weighs half a ton, his arm has a striking power of over 650 lbs. You'd better keep your mouth shut, Kostenko. You're new here, you don't know anything."

"I have it," said Nikolai Petrovich firmly. "This is what we'll do. I'll phone the hostel and get the student workers out. You, Ryabkin, get along to the car park. Blast it! They'll all be at the club, it's Saturday! Never mind, run and find

90

three chauffeurs anyway. We must get out the caterpillar bulldozers. Right, Piskunov?"

"That's all right, and get a move on. Only. . . ."

"You get off to the institute, Piskunov. Locate Urm and phone back at once to the car park. Kostenko, you go with him. And look sharp, comrades. The devil, if we can only stop him getting past the gates!"

They all rushed out, pulling on their overcoats as they went. Ryabkin stumbled and rammed his head into Kostenko's back, so that he fell flat on all fours.

"Blast it!"

"What's the matter? Lost your spectacles?"

"No, it's all right."

A ferocious wind swept clouds of dry snow over the ground; it whined piteously in the telephone wires, whistled loudly in the ironwork of the high voltage pylons. Soft yellow rectangles of light fell from the cottage windows on to the snow-drifts. Everything else was plunged in impenetrable darkness.

"Well, I'm off," said Ryabkin. "Mind how you go, you chaps, don't take unnecessary risks."

He stumbled and fell again. For a short time he was floundering in a snow-drift, swearing at the snow-storm, cursing Urm and everybody concerned in the unfortunate occurrence. Then his light fur coat showed up by the wicket-gate and then disappeared in gusts of whirling snow.

Piskunov and Kostenko made for the high road.

"I can't see what use the tractors will be," mumbled Kostenko.

"What suggestion have you to offer, then?" asked Piskunov.

"I don't mean that . . . I simply don't understand. D'you want to destroy your Urm?"

Piskunov heaved a sigh.

"We want to bring Urm to a standstill," he said.

He gathered up the tail of his overcoat and scrambled through a snow-drift. Kostenko followed, embarrassed and forlorn. Ahead lay a snow-covered field, beyond it—the high road. The power-station stood on the opposite side of the high road. Piskunov chose the short cut across open ground where the earth had been excavated the previous autumn in preparation for a new building. Kostenko heard him swearing to himself as he stumbled over a heap of ice-covered bricks and metal reinforcement rods. It was hard going. The chain of lights shining from the institute windows was scarcely visible through the blanket of snow.

"Let's wait a bit," said Kostenko, finally. "By God, it's heavy going. We'll have a breather."

Piskunov squatted beside him. What really could have happened? He knew Urm better than anyone else in the institute. Every screw, every electrode, every lens of the magnificent mechanism had passed through his hands. He had reckoned he could calculate and foretell every one of his movements in every possible circumstance. And now, look what had happened! Urm had "voluntarily" got out of his cellar and was promenading round the power-station. Why?

Urm's behaviour was determined by his "brain," an extraordinarily complicated, delicate apparatus of germanium, spongy platinum and ferrite. An ordinary computor has tens of thousands of triggers, elementary organs which receive, store and give out signals; but Urm's "brain" was operated by about eighteen million logical cells. Reactions to numerous situations, different variants of changes of circumstances were "programmed" on them; fulfilment of a vast number of different operations was provided for. What could have influenced the "brain," the programme? Radiation from the atomic motor? No, the motor was surrounded by a powerful screen of zirconium, gadolinium and boron-steel. In practice, not a single neutron, not a single energy quantum of gamma-rays could penetrate this screen. Could the receptors be at fault, then? No, the receptors had been in perfect order only this very evening. Hence it could only have been the "brain" itself. The programme? The new, complicated programme for which Piskunov himself had been responsible?... The programming ... that was it!

Slowly Piskunov rose to his feet.

"A spontaneous reflex!" he declared. "Of course, it's a spontaneous reflex! Idiot!"

Kostenko glanced at him, horrified.

"I don't get your meaning."

"But I do. It's obvious. Yet who would have thought of it? Everything was going so well."

"Look over there!" cried Kostenko, jumping to his feet.

A flickering blue flare illuminated the grey-black sky over the institute and against this background the silhouettes of dark buildings, surprisingly clear-cut and yet somehow unreal, emerged from the whirling snow-storm. The thin chain of lights which marked the boundaries of the institute blinked and then died out.

"That's the transformer gone!" said Piskunov huskily. "The sub-station is exactly opposite the reactor tower! Urm's there.... But what about the guards...?"

"Come on, let's run!" suggested Kostenko.

Together they ran forward, but it was not so easy. In the teeth of the wind, they floundered in snow-concealed ruts, fell down, picked themselves up only to fall down again.

"Come on, hurry!" urged Piskunov.

His agitation and the biting wind drew tears from his eyes. They trickled down his face, froze in icicles on his eyelashes, making it difficult to see. He grabbed Kostenko by the arm and dragged him along, still muttering hoarsely: "Hurry, hurry!"

The flash over the institute had evidently been seen in the settlement. A siren was whining the alarm, lights sprang up in the cottages where the guards lived, the blinding shaft of a searchlight swept the field. Out of the gloom it picked up the snow-drifts, the latticed pylons of the high-tension wires, glided over the brick wall surrounding the institute and then pin-pointed the gate. Small black figures were moving hurriedly by the gates.

"Who's that, over there?" asked Kostenko, panting.

"The guards, probably the militia, too." Piskunov stopped and rubbed his eyes.

"The gates... they've shut them," he said with a break in his voice. "Good fellows! That means Urm's still there."

Clearly everyone had now been alerted. Already the beams from three searchlights were probing along the institute walls. Snow-flakes danced in the blue light. Through the noise and howling of wind, there was shouting; someone swore angrily. At last there came a roar of engines and clanking of caterpillar tracks. The gigantic bulldozer tractors were rolling out from the car park.

"Kostenko, look!" said Piskunov. "Watch closely. We are now witnessing the most extraordinary raid in the history of mankind. Watch closely!"

Kostenko looked sideways at Piskunov. It appeared to him that tears were streaming down the engineer's face; they could have been due to the wind.

Meanwhile the clanking of caterpillar tracks no longer came from behind, but were to the right of them. The tractors had reached the high road. The shaking headlights were just distinguishable, showing that there were five tractors.

"Five against one," whispered Piskunov. "He hasn't a chance in a million. His bump of spontaneity won't help here."

Suddenly there was a different atmosphere which, at first, Kostenko could not explain to himself. The snow-storm was still raging, clouds of dry snow were still sweeping the ground, the tractor engines were still roaring menacingly and relentlessly. But there were no searchlights playing over the field. They were fixed on the gates. The gates were ajar and there was no one standing by.

"What the devil!" exclaimed Kostenko.

"He couldn't, surely...."

Piskunov did not stop to finish the sentence. Without another word, they rushed together towards the institute. When only a couple of hundred paces separated them from the gates, Piskunov who was in the lead encountered a man with a rifle. The man yelled in horror and was about to make off, but Piskunov caught him fast by the shoulder.

"Now, what's up?" he asked.

The militiaman looked from side to side with a frightened expression, then swore and pulled himself together.

"He's got out!" he declared. "Got away. Knocked down the gates and simply went out. He almost trampled Makeyev down. I'm going to the settlement for help."

"Which way did he go?"

The militiaman waved his arm vaguely to the left.

"That way, I think.... Along the high road."

"Then he'll meet the tractors. Come on."

What happened in the next minute was something he never forgot to the end of his days. Something enormous and shapeless emerged suddenly coming towards them out of the whirling, snowy darkness, red and green lights blinked straight into their eyes, and a sharp unmodulated voice spoke.

"Good day, how are you?"

"Urm, stop!" shrieked Piskunov in desperation.

Kostenko watched the militiaman run off, saw Piskunov raise his arms and shake his fists as the gigantic figure enveloped in steam, the sinister dummy, moved past him, lifting up its thick, log-like legs, and vanished into the snow-storm.

3

Urm carefully closed the door behind him, as he always did if the door was not smashed down; he stepped forward and stopped. All round him were sounds, movements, rays. The night shone in an enchanting, coloured kaleidoscope of radio-waves. About 40 feet ahead of him stood a low building with wide, iron-barred windows. Its walls sent out bright infra-red light. A low, powerful humming came from the building. Millions of snow-flakes circled in the air, settling on Urm's metal-plated body, which was warmed by the heat from his atomic motor, then immediately melting and evaporating.

Urm turned his head and decided that the nearest, most interesting object of investigation could only be this low building standing opposite him. He found the entrance at once by following the path on the leeward side. Low fir-trees grew round the building and he stopped briefly to break off one of them and study it. Then he opened the door and went in.

Two men were seated at a table in the narrow little room; when they caught sight of him they jumped up horrified and glared at him. Urm closed the door behind him (he even let down the latch) and confronted them.

"How do you do?" he asked.

"Where's Comrade Piskunov?" asked one of the men, mystified.

"Comrade Piskunov has gone out. What message shall I give him?" replied Urm, indifferently.

He was not interested in the people. His attention had been drawn to a small shaggy creature huddled in the corner against the wall. "Warm, alive, has a strong smell, not a man," was Urm's definition of it.

"Good day, how do you do?" said Urm, addressing the creature.

"Gr-r-r-r," replied the creature with the courage of desperation; it bared its sharp, white teeth and huddled closer into the corner.

Urm was so engrossed in the dog that he totally ignored the fact that the militiamen had cunningly barricaded themselves behind the table and cupboard and were hurriedly unfastening their holsters.

Whining piteously, the little dog slipped past Urm, its tail between his legs. But Urm was far more agile than the dog; he was more agile than the most agile animal on earth. Like lightning his trunk silently made a half-turn, his long arm stretched out like a telescope and his hand spanned the little dog's back. Simultaneously a shot rang out: one of the militiamen's nerves were all to pieces. The bullet resounded against the armour-plate covering Urm's back and ricochetted into the wall. Some plaster fell down.

"Stop that, Sidorenko!" yelled the other militiaman.

Urm let the shivering dog go and stared at the pale but very determined men with their revolvers ready for action. He sniffed with curiosity. An unfamiliar smell of smokeless powder filled the air. The dog crouched at the feet of the militiamen, but Urm was no longer interested in it. Turning, he moved towards the next door on which was emblazoned a skull and cross-bones, struck through with the jagged red line of lightning. Struck dumb with astonishment, the militiamen watched his pincer-like fingers fumbling at the wards of the lock. The door opened. Recovering themselves, the men rushed after him.

"Stop! Go back!" they cried.

They clung to his armoured sides, forgetting all else in their horror at the thought of the damage the iron monster could do to the transformer. But Urm simply ignored them. Their efforts did not make the slightest impression on him. They might just as well have tried to stop a moving tractor. One of them pushed the other aside and fired twice point blank at Urm's head. The brightly-lit room of the sub-station resounded with the noise of the shots.

Urm staggered. The ebonite shell of the right acoustic receptor was shattered to pieces. The bent horn of the locator was broken off and hung loosely on its flex. A crash of broken glass came from the ceiling.

Urm had never before experienced attack. He had no instinct of self-preservation; he had had no experience, nor could he have had, of fighting against people. But Urm was capable of comparing facts, drawing logical conclusions and selecting a line of behaviour that would give him the maximum safety. It took only a fraction of a second to perform these thought operations. The next moment he had turned round and moved towards the men, his terrible pincers menacingly extended.

The militiamen separated: one ran behind the switchboard, the other jumped behind the massive steel casing of the nearest transformer, hurriedly reloading his revolver.

"Sidorenko! Run to the office, get on the phone and give the alarm," he shouted.

But it was not possible for Sidorenko to get to the door. Urm moved much faster than a man, and the militiaman had scarcely showed himself from behind the switchboard, before Urm had taken two steps and was confronting him. The men then decided to make a joint attempt at escape. This failed, too. Urm rushed from the switchboard to the transformer with the speed of an express train.

The switchboard was split in half when Urm clumsily lurched against it and the wind whistled through the bullet holes in the windows and glass ceiling.

Finally Urm tired of the game and decided to leave the men in peace. Standing in front of the transformer, he deliberately placed his arms under the casing. Using this opportunity, the militiamen fled headlong to the office. At the same moment there came a deafening crash, a blinding blue flash lit up everything all round, and then there was total darkness. An acrid smell of burning metal, smoke and hot varnish burst from the room. Deafened and crushed, the militiamen did not at once realise what had happened. Then heavy steps shook the floor of the office and a gruff voice spoke through the darkness.

"Good day, how do you do?"

The latch clicked. The creaking door opened, for a second the outline of the ponderous iron monster showed up in the dim rectangle, then the door closed again.

Urm paced across the grounds of the institute, lifting his legs up in the air and sinking deep into the snow. The institute was completely plunged in darkness, and even Urm's infra-red sight gave him little assistance. He could only distinguish a feeble glow round his own stomach and legs, where snow-flakes were melting and evaporating. A few feebly phosphorescent silhouettes of men flitted between the buildings. Urm ignored them. Orientating himself by the instructions of his locator, although one of its horns had been shot off and it was now impossible to determine distances correctly, Urm went on.

He was particularly interested in the distant lights of the

settlement which was hardly visible through the snow-storm. It was from there that the bright blue beams of the searchlights shone out. He went as far as the wall, hesitated, then turned to the left. He knew quite well that there are always doors in walls. Soon he found himself at the gates. They were large, iron gates. More important, however, was the fact that they were bolted. Voices, raised in alarm, were audible beyond the gates, through a chink in which a bright blue light was shining.

"Good day," growled Urm and pushed against the gates. They resisted him; they were firmly bolted. From somewhere in the distance came a sound of clanking metal. Something very interesting was happening on the other side of the gates. Urm pressed harder, then he drew back, threw back his head and made a rush at the gates, striking them with his armoured breast. The voices on the other side of the gates were silenced. Then someone cried out, falteringly:

"Get back. Hi, there! Don't shoot at the devil!"

"Good day, how do you do?" said Urm, then made another rush and struck again. The gates crumpled. The bolts appeared to be stronger than the hinges in the concrete wall, for the gates lay flat on the snow like duck-boards. Urm walked over them, past the fleeing militiamen and plunged into the snow-storm raging in the open field.

He strode forward, hardly able to keep his equilibrium on the uneven ground covered with an undulating sea of dry snow. At one point he found nothing under his foot and he fell to the ground. The snow sizzled under him. He had never fallen down before, yet the next moment he had his arms pressed against the ground, stretched to their full extent, and was drawing up his legs under him.

Once more on his feet, he stood still looking round. Ahead glimmered the lights from the cottages. To the left, three human figures loomed out of the darkness; farther away a chain of bulldozers with engines roaring were driving towards the gates. Urm turned to the left. As he walked past the men, he greeted them and at once recognised one of them as the Master. The Master could deprive him of the possibility of moving. Urm remembered that perfectly well and began to walk faster. The Master was lost in the whirling snow-storm behind him.

He came to a flat, smooth patch of ground. A bright light illuminated him from head to foot. Cumbersome, metal monsters with heavy shields in front of them were rolling towards him; they came to a halt, snorting angrily.

Urm stood five paces away from the leading bulldozer, slowly turning his round head from side to side and repeating the words:

"Good day, how do you do?"

4

Nikolai Petrovich jumped down from the tractor.

"Where are you off to?" yelled the driver, terrified.

Then Piskunov appeared on the road. Dishevelled, his hair standing on end (his cap lay somewhere in the open field), his hands plunged in the pockets of his unbuttoned coat, he walked round the bulldozer and stood in front of Urm. Not more than five paces separated them. Urm towered over the engineer, his faceted sides gleamed in the headlights, his steam-enveloped stomach was glossy and damp; his round head with the narrow glass eyes, the alerted ears of the receptors and the horn of the locator looked like the horrible, comic mask of a pumpkin, the sort the village lads use to terrify the girls. His head swayed rhythmically and his eyes watched Piskunov's every movement.

"Urm!" shouted Piskunov at him.

Urm stopped moving his head, his articulated arms pressed close to his body.

"Urm, obey my order!"

"I am ready," replied Urm.

Someone laughed nervously.

Piskunov stepped forward and placed his gloved hand on Urm's chest. Swiftly his fingers ran over the armour, probing for the most important thing—the switch that connected the calculating and analysing part of Urm's brain with the power and movement system. Then something strange occurred, something that only Piskunov had expected and feared most of all. Evidently some association connecting the Master's gesture with a sudden inability to move was preserved in Urm's memory. Piskunov's fingers had scarcely touched the switch when Urm turned sharply. His armoured arm passed swiftly over Piskunov's head as he succeeded in jumping aside; then he began to move in leisurely fashion back along the high road. Nikolai Petrovich was the first to come to his senses.

"Hi, you fellows!" he cried out. "Drive the bulldozers to the right and left! Cut him off from the road to the gates. Piskunov! Hi, Piskunov!"

But Piskunov was deaf to his shouts. While the bulldozers were manoeuvring along both sides of the road, he plunged into the snow-drifts, hurrying after Urm.

"Stop, Urm!" he shouted in a high-pitched, broken voice. "Stop, you swine! Come back!"

He was completely out of breath. But Urm walked faster and faster and the distance between them gradually increased. In the end Piskunov stopped, thrust his hands into his pockets, hunched up his shoulders and watched him disappearing in the distance. Nikolai Petrovich and Ryabkin hurried up to him, Kostenko came last.

"Where d'you think you're off to?" asked Nikolai Petro-vich, angrily.

Piskunov did not reply.

"He won't obey," he finally muttered. "Don't you see, Nikolai? He won't obey. It's obviously a spontaneous reflex."

Nikolai Petrovich nodded.

"I thought as much."

"I should think so!" ejaculated Ryabkin. "You might just as well allow a train to choose its own route and schedule."

"What is this spontaneous reflex?" asked Kostenko timor-ously.

He got no reply.

"And yet, in spite of everything, it's a remarkable thing, I must say." Nikolai Petrovich blew his nose and stuffed the handkerchief back in his pocket. "He won't obey! Then we'll have to. . . ."

"Come on, let's go!" said Piskunov resolutely.

Meanwhile the bulldozers had formed a semi-circle, and they began to surround Urm as he stumped leisurely along the road. One of them rolled on to the road ahead of him, its stern towards the gates; another was overtaking him from behind; the rest were closing in on the sides, two to the left, one to the right. For some time Urm had noticed that he was being surrounded but probably attached no importance to the fact. On he went down the road until his chest touched the front bulldozer. The tractor shook slightly from the im-pact, the driver, his face tense, grabbed the levers. Urm moved back a step and made another rush. Iron clanged against iron, flying sparks amid the snow-flakes glittered in the beam of the headlights. In a trice the bulldozer behind was press-ing into Urm's back. He stood stockstill, his head slowly re-volving round its axis like a schoolroom globe. Micromanipulators extended like black snakes from his breastplate and hurriedly fumbled at the upper edge of the iron shield and were concealed again. Two more bulldozers drew up on either side of him, firmly cutting off the last lines of retreat. Urm was a prisoner.

"Comrade engineers! Comrade Piskunov! What shall I do next?" shouted the driver of the first machine.

"Comrade Piskunov has gone out. What message shall I give him?" came Urm's reply.

He made a flourish with his arm and struck the bulldozer. Then he struck again and again, rhythmically, bending slightly at each blow, like a boxer training. Sheafs of sparks flew out with each clang from the metal-fingered fists.

Piskunov, Nikolai Petrovich, Ryabkin and Kostenko all rushed up.

"We've got to do something immediately, otherwise he'll cripple himself," said Ryabkin, alarmed.

Without a word Piskunov climbed on the tractor tracks, while Ryabkin, seizing him by the coat, tried to drag him back.

"What the hell?" cried Piskunov, angrily.

"Look here, you're the only one who knows Urm down to the minutest detail of his mechanism. Suppose he crushes you . . . this whole business may go on for months. Someone else had better do the job."

"Quite right," agreed Nikolai Petrovich. "I'll go."

One of the workers approached the engineers.

"Perhaps you'd pick one of us," he suggested. "We're younger, more agile. . . ."

"I'll do it," said Kostenko, frowning.

Nikolai Petrovich looked at them all, with a smile.

"And which of you knows what to do?"

There was no reply.

"There, you see. I'm the only one who knows what to do. And if something ... if I ... then get the laboratory workers on the job. But don't let Piskunov get near him."

He threw off his overcoat and scrambled on to the tractor. Piskunov tore himself away from Ryabkin.

"Let go, Ryabkin! What rubbish! I'll do it myself...."

Ryabkin was silenced. But Kostenko took a firm hold of Piskunov's shoulder on the other side. Piskunov bit his lip and stood silent, watching Nikolai Petrovich.

By now Urm was in a frenzy. The lower part of his body was held in the firm grip of the bulldozers, but the upper part could move freely; he was turning with lightning speed from one side to the other, his steel fists battering at the iron shield. Puffs of steam circled round him in the dense snow. "Striking power of the fist—650 lbs," Kostenko recalled.

Gritting his teeth, Nikolai Petrovich crouched between the bulldozers at Urm's feet waiting for the right moment. His ears ached from the clanging and banging. He knew Urm had noticed him, for the glass eyes, alert and shining, kept turning towards him.

"Keep still, be still," whispered Nikolai Petrovich. "Urm, little dove, keep still! Quiet now, you scoundrel!"

A different noise sounded through the blows, something cracked, either Urm's strong arm or the iron shield of the bulldozer. Not another second must be lost. He dived under Urm's fist and pressed close to his side. Then Urm filled everyone with astonishment. His arms dropped loosely. The clatter ceased; once more the howling of the snow-storm across the field and the rattle of the tractor engines could be heard. Pale and sweating Nikolai Petrovich straightened up and put his hand on Urm's chest. There was a hollow click. The green and red lights on Urm's shoulders were extinguished.

"It's all over," whispered Piskunov, and closed his eyes.

Everyone began talking loudly, there was laughter and joking. The drivers helped Nikolai Petrovich to scramble out from beneath Urm, holding him in their arms. Piskunov embraced him.

"Now for the institute," he said jerkily. "We've work to do. We'll need a week or a month. We've got to knock the nonsense out of him and make a real Urm of him—a Universal Robot Machine."

6

"What actually did happen to Urm?" asked Kostenko. "And what exactly is a spontaneous reflex?"

Tired and drowsy after the sleepless night, Nikolai Petrovich began to explain.

"Well, you see, Urm was designed to the order of the Interplanetary Communications Board. He is different from other cybernetic machines, even the most complicated, because he is intended for work in conditions which even the greatest programme genius cannot exactly foresee. For example, who knows what the conditions on Venus are like? It may be covered with oceans. Or deserts perhaps, or jungles, or boiling pitch. It is impossible, too dangerous, to send people there as yet. Urms, dozens of them, will be sent. But what programmes should be fed to them? The whole trouble is that at the present level of cybernetics, it is not yet possible to teach the machine to 'think' abstractly. . . ."

"And what does that mean?"

"Well, just imagine that we are sending a cybernetic machine to investigate some unknown locality: to find out the nature of the soil, the presence of minerals, the flora and fauna, etc. The machine is given the task of encircling the locality, then crossing it from north to south. If we know that the locality is as level as a table, the cybernetic structure can be perfectly simple. One or two receptors, a gyrocompass, a few relays.... Tens of thousands of such mechanisms are in operation on tractors and automatic combines in the fields of the state farms. But that is only where the locality is relatively level and, so to speak, without any snags. But what if we don't know what it is like? If there happen to be ravines, rivers with deep pools, swamps? Then our machine runs the risk of getting smashed up, drowned or bogged down. To be ready for such possibilities the machine has to be provided with a more complicated 'brain,' it has to be given a more elaborate programme. For instance, it is possible to 'teach' the machine to find where rivers can be forded, to prohibit it from going into deep places or from approaching the edge of a precipice. It can be taught to avoid obstacles or, if possible, to overcome them, using various devices in the nature of a powerful system of equilibrium, as with our Urm, or like his arms and legs.... Actually that is why we gave Urm arms and legs; wheels and caterpillar tracks are by no means suitable everywhere."

"That's quite clear," interrupted Kostenko, impatiently. "What I'm interested in is...."

"Now, look here," continued Nikolai Petrovich, unperturbed. "Suppose we feed a programme of behaviour to the machine to use in an encounter with a wall. The machine has to avoid the wall. But we did not take into account that the locality might be thickly wooded. The machine 'takes' the forest for a wall and starts to avoid it, and yet it could easily pass straight through it."

"Obviously," remarked Kostenko.

"Or, fearing the machine might be submerged in a swamp, we 'teach' it to avoid marshy places. And then the machine retreats from a harmless ploughed field, from sand or peatland. We had to 'teach' the machine to be able to act in every situation, even the most fantastic conditions of which we, who draw up the programmes, have no idea at all. The machine had to acquire new properties to take the place of the capacity to 'understand' that although bushes may resemble a wall they are nevertheless penetrable. That although a swamp may produce the signal 'the soil is not firm,' this signal is produced not only by a swamp. In short, the machine had to learn to go beyond single logical connections of the type 'soil that is not firm means a swamp' and 'a barrier impenetrable to light means a wall.' But how can the machine be 'taught' this? And so Piskunov suggested creating a self-programming machine. Urm's 'brain' was given a programme, which consisted essentially in an endeavour to fill in the vacant cells of the memory. In other words, Urm was imbued with a 'passion' for experiment, a passion to learn about what is new. This programme (we call it the internal programme) was superimposed on the basic one and worked in co-operation with it. Piskunov calculated that when Urm came up against some new, unforeseen factor, he would not retreat from it, would not pass it by indifferently, but, within the framework of the possibilities allowed by the basic programme, would investigate this new thing and either overcome it, if it could be overcome, or use it in the interests of the basic programme. That is to say, Urm would select without the help of man the most suitable type of behaviour for every new event. This is the most perfect model of consciousness in the world. But the result was unexpected. I mean, theoretically we admitted such a phenomenon, but in practice ... well. ... Briefly, the combination of the internal programme with the basic one produced thousands of new unforeseen possibilities of the machine's reaction to external influences. Piskunov christened them spontaneous reflexes. These spontaneously arising small programmes forgot, if one can put it that way, the basic programme; the internal programme became the decisive one, and Urm began to 'act of his own accord.' "

"And what's to be done now?"

"We'll try some other line." Nikolai Petrovich stretched himself and yawned. "We shall perfect the analysing capacities of the 'brain,' and the receptor system...."

"But what about the spontaneous reflex? Isn't anyone interested in it?"

"Aha! Piskunov had already thought of something. In short, Urm will all the same be the first to set foot on the unexplored planets and to go down to the unexplored depths of oceans. People will not have to take the risk.... Listen here, Kostenko, let's turn in now, shall we? You'll be working with us and learning all about it, I give you my word."

ALEXANDER KAZANTSEV
A VISITOR FROM OUTER SPACE*

"We'll be having a get-together with the scientists this evening," Boris Yefimovich informed me one day.

I knew that besides Nizovsky, the paleontologist, we also had on board a geographer named Vasilyev, who was in charge of an expedition to the distant archipelago.

Then there was an astronomer on the ship too. He had come aboard while the *Georgy Sedov* was lying off Ustye, delivering some dinghies to an unfortunate captain who had lost his ship's boats in a storm. I had gone on deck early that morning to catch a glimpse, even from a distance, of the mainland. We had not sighted land for several months. And now ... there it was on the horizon, just a narrow, hazy strip. Yet it was the coastline of the Great Continent.

A motor boat was ploughing its way towards us, across waters orange-tinted as the sky at dawn.

"More passengers," remarked the first mate, who was supervising the lowering of the dinghies. "Three members of an astronomical expedition."

"An astronomical expedition, here in the North? Whatever for?"

---

* The scientific information and hypotheses put forward by the astronomer formed the subject of a discussion at a meeting of the Astronomical Society in Moscow on February 20, 1948. The discussion has continued in the press to this day.

The first mate offered no explanation.

The motor boat drew alongside and three people climbed the rope ladder. The first was short, big-boned and lean, with an angular, sun-tanned face. He wore horn-rimmed spectacles and his bulging forehead gave him a rather queer expression. I noticed the slight slant of his unusually elongated eyes.

He bowed to me very politely while still some distance away and then came up and introduced himself.

"Yevgeny Alexeich Krymov, astronomer. We're making a high-latitude expedition. And this is Natasha, I mean Natalya Georgiyevna Glagoleva, botanist."

A girl wearing a padded cotton jacket and trousers gave me a feeble handshake. She had dark rings round her eyes and seemed exhausted. Netayev, the bosun's mate, took her at once to the cabin prepared for her.

The third passenger was a young man, scarcely more than a lad. With an air of importance he was supervising the raising of their luggage from the motor launch.

Is Life Possible on Other Planets?

Yes, it is possible. The idea of a multitude of populated worlds was first put forward by Giordano Bruno in the Middle Ages. For this idea the scientist was burned at the stake by the obscurantists of Rome on February 17, 1600, on the Square of Flowers.

The materialist conception of the universe is in accord with the origin and development of life on other planets wherever conditions are favourable.

The necessary conditions for the existence of the forms of life known to us are, first and foremost: a temperature of not more than $+100°C$ and not below $-100°C$; the presence of carbon, which is one of the chief component parts of the structure of living organisms; the presence of oxygen, which plays the chief part in the

"Be careful, now. They're instruments, scientific equipment!" he was shouting. "Look out, can't you understand? They're fragile instruments!"

At length all the equipment lay on deck. I saw nothing at all that resembled a telescope.

What could an astronomical expedition be doing in the Arctic? Surely the stars were not more visible from here. Profiting from the fact that the ship was at anchor in the port of Diky Island, Boris Yefimovich invited his scientist guests into the saloon.

Katya, the buffet girl, brought out smoked sprats from some secret supply, and the captain's personal brandy made its appearance on the table.

---

vital energy reactions of the living organism; the presence of water and, finally, the absence in the planet's atmosphere of poisonous gases.

All these conditions can be observed only in exceptional cases, when sought for in the universe among the countless stars and possible planetary systems. But it is precisely this countless number of the stars and their possible planets that greatly increases the probability of all these conditions occurring in thousands, and perhaps millions, of places in the universe.

We are particularly interested in our neighbours—the planets of our own solar system. The conditions which exist on their surface can be established by us with a fair degree of accuracy.

Of all the planets of the solar system, the giant planets must at once be excluded from those which may have life on them; for instance, there are Saturn, Jupiter, Uranus and Neptune. They are covered with eternal ice and surrounded by poisonous atmospheres. On the planet farthest removed from the Sun, Pluto, there is eternal night and intolerable frost; on Mercury, which is nearest to the Sun, there is no air. One side of it is always turned to the Sun and is scorched, the other is plunged in eternal darkness and cosmic cold.

The most favourable for the origin of life are three planets: the Earth, Venus and Mars.

The scientists, including botanist Natasha, now rosy-cheeked and alert after her sleep, cheerfully did justice to food and drink.

"Tell me," I asked Krymov, "what exactly is the object of your astronomical expedition?"

"To establish the existence of life on Mars," replied Krymov, helping himself to fish. I almost shot out of my chair.

"On Mars? You're joking!"

Krymov looked at me in surprise through his round spectacles.

"Why should I be joking?"

"Can you really make observations of Mars in these parts?" I asked.

"No, at this time of year Mars is not usually clearly visible."

The temperature conditions on all three planets do not exceed those at which life is possible. Venus and Mars, like the Earth, have an atmosphere.

It is difficult to judge of the composition of Venus's atmosphere, as the planet is enveloped in an unbroken covering of clouds. Still, poisonous gases have been discovered in the upper strata of the atmosphere. Evidently Venus's atmosphere is extremely rich in carbon dioxide, which is fatal to animals, but is an excellent medium for the development of lower plants.

The existence of incipient life on Venus is not out of the question, but so far cannot be proved.

The question is quite different with the Earth's other neighbour, Mars.

What Exactly Is Mars?

Mars is a planet about half the size of the Earth. It is one and a half times farther from the Sun than the Earth is.

It takes Mars 24 hours 37 minutes to revolve round its axis.

Its axis is inclined towards the plane of the orbit to approximately the same extent as the Earth's. Consequently the seasons of the year on Mars are the same as on the Earth.

It has been established that Mars is surrounded by an atmosphere,

8—1316   *113*

"You're suggesting that these people intend to study Mars in the Arctic, without even looking at the sky?" I persisted.

"Our study of Mars is being made at the Alma-Ata Observatory, but up here. . . ."

"Well, what about here?"

"We're looking for proof of the existence of life on Mars."

"That's most interesting!" exclaimed Nizovsky. "Ever since I was a child I've been interested in the canals on Mars! Schiaparelli, Lowell, weren't they the scientists who made a study of Mars?"

"Tikhov," added Krymov, didactically. "Gavriil Andrianovich Tikhov."

---

and no gases harmful to the development of life have been discovered in it.

There is approximately the same quantity of carbon dioxide on Mars as there is on the Earth. The oxygen there is probably about one-hundredth of the amount to be found in the Earth's atmosphere.

The climate of Mars is harsh and severe, as described accurately in the story.

Mars is the same age, and has passed through all the same phases of development as the Earth.

During the period of its cooling and the formation of the first oceans, it was covered with unbroken cloud, just as Venus is today and as the Earth was during the carboniferous period.

During this "warm" period of the planet's development the temperature on the surface of Mars did not depend on the Sun as was the case with the Earth at that time. Conditions on Mars then were in all respects similar to those on the Earth and, as we know, they were favourable to the appearance of life in the primitive oceans.

A similar process could also have taken place on Mars.

In the warm period, the first plants, like the horse-tails of the carboniferous period, and other primitive forms of life, were able to develop.

"He founded the new science—astrobotany!" explained the young woman brightly.

"Astrobotany?" I queried. "Astra—a star ... and then botany? I can't see the connection."

Natasha burst out laughing.

"Of course there's such a thing as astrobotany!" she declared. "The science of vegetation on other planets!"

"On Mars," interjected Krymov.

"At the Academy of the Kazakh S.S.R. we now have a department of this new Soviet science, astrobotany," Natasha proudly explained.

Only in the periods that followed, when the cloud covering had dispersed, did Mars, which had a smaller gravitational force than the Earth, lose the particles of the atmosphere which had been trying to break away from it, and acquire conditions on its surface which differed from those of the Earth.

However, living organisms could have adapted themselves to these new conditions in the process of evolution.

Besides losing its atmosphere, Mars also lost water, which evaporated into the atmosphere and was carried away into space in the form of vapour.

Gradually Mars became transformed into a planet covered with waterless deserts.

Today dark patches, once called seas, are discernible on its surface. But if in ancient times Mars did have seas, it has long ago lost them. No astronomer has ever observed the kind of light patches which would be noticeable on the surface of water. The areas of Mars close to the poles are covered alternately with a substance which, judging by its reflecting power, resembles our terrestrial ice.

As the Sun's rays warm one or other of the polar regions the size of this white cap (G. A. Tikhov's more precise investigations have shown that it is green), resembling ice without a covering of snow, diminishes and it becomes encircled by a dark strip (apparently damp soil).

"What's this I hear? Astronomers, and in the Arctic?" asked the captain.

"You see, it's like this," began Krymov. "We've got to find conditions similar to those which exist on Mars. It's one and a half times farther from the sun than the Earth. Its atmosphere is as rarefied as it is here at a height of fifteen kilometres. The climate there is harsh and severe."

"Just think," intervened Natasha, "at the Equator it is 20°C above zero in the daytime and —70°C at night."

"Tough going," remarked the captain.

"In the middle zone," Krymov continued, "it is 80°C be-

When cooling takes place, the ice cap of the planet begins to enlarge, while the dark border round it ceases to be visible. This has led to the conclusion that the water vapour present in a small quantity in the atmosphere of Mars falls in the form of snow in the polar regions and covers the soil there with a layer of ice about four inches thick.

As the warming process takes place, the ice melts and the water formed either soaks into the soil or is spread by some method over the planet.

It occurs in turn at each pole of Mars. When the ice melts near the south pole, it is formed at the north pole and vice versa.

What Exactly Is Astrobotany?

This is a new Soviet science created by one of our most outstanding astronomers, Gavriil Andrianovich Tikhov, Corresponding Member of the U.S.S.R. Academy of Sciences.

Tikhov was the first scientist to take photographs of Mars through a coloured light filter. By this means he was able to establish the exact colouring of various parts of the planet at different seasons of the year.

Of particular interest were the patches which were once called seas. These patches changed colour from a greenish-blue tint in the spring to a light brown in the summer and a dark-brown tone in the winter. Tikhov drew a parallel between these changes on

low zero day and night in the winter (and the seasons on Mars are the same as here on the Earth)."

"Like it is in the Turukhansk Territory," added the geographer, speaking for the first time.

"Yes, the climate on Mars is severe. But don't we have similar temperatures here in the Arctic?" Krymov liked to talk about it. He was clearly devoted to his astrobotany.

"Now I see why you are here," said the captain.

"And there is life in the Arctic," continued the astronomer. "And there are even more favourable conditions on Mars, too. In the polar circles, for instance, where the sun does not set for many months on end, the temperature remains at about

---

Mars and the change in the colouring of the evergreen taiga in Siberia. Green in the spring or a hazy blue, the taiga turns brown in the summer and in the winter-time takes on a dark-brown hue.

At the same time the colouring of the vast expanses of Mars remain an unchanged reddish-brown, similar in all respects to the colouring of the deserts of the Earth.

The idea that the changing colouring of the patches on Mars are zones of unbroken vegetation required to be proved.

Attempts by means of the spectroscope to discover chlorophyll on Mars, the presence of which would ensure photosynthesis and living of land plants, have not been successful.

As described in the story, it is characteristic of the Earth's plants that when photographed in infra-red rays they appear white on the prints, as though covered with snow. If the zones of supposed vegetation on Mars appeared similarly white on photographs in infra-red rays, there would be no doubt about there being vegetation on Mars.

However, new photographs of Mars did not confirm these bold assumptions.

But this did not dismay G. A. Tikhov. He made a comparative investigation of the reflecting properties of land plants in the South and North.

The results were astounding. On the photographs in infra-red heat rays, only those plants which reflected infra-red heat rays

15°C above zero day and night. Excellent conditions for vegetation!"

"Then there really is vegetation on Mars?" I could not refrain from asking.

"So far we have had no direct proofs," replied Krymov, evasively.

The captain poured out a round of brandy.

"Astronomy is certainly a fine profession. We sailors and polar explorers have a habit of talking about ourselves. Now perhaps you, comrade geographer, and you, Nizovsky, and particularly our astronomer friends might like to tell us how you came to be scientists," suggested Boris Yefimovich.

---

without utilising them appeared to be white. In the North the plants (for example, cloudberries and mosses) did not reflect, but absorbed the heat rays, which were by no means superfluous for them. In the photographs in infra-red rays, the northern plants did not come out white, just as the zones of supposed vegetation on Mars did not appear white on the prints.

This investigation, strengthened by polar and high-mountain expeditions which Tikhov's pupils undertook, led him to the clever conclusion that plants, in adapting themselves to their conditions of existence, acquire the ability to absorb the rays they need and to reflect those they do not need. In the South, where there is a great deal of sun, plants do not require the heat rays of the spectrum and reflect them; in the North, which has little warmth from the sun, plants cannot allow themselves this luxury, and so they try to absorb all the rays of the solar spectrum. On Mars, where the climate is particularly severe and the sun is not strong, plants would naturally try to absorb as many rays as possible, and the failure to compare the plants of Mars, in this particular respect, with the southern plants of the Earth is quite understandable. They more resemble the plants of the Arctic.

In arriving at this conclusion, Tikhov also found the cause of the failure to discover chlorophyll on Mars.

Further study of this question forced Tikhov more and more to

"What's there to tell," replied Nizovsky. "I went to school, then to university, then stayed on as a post-graduate research student, and that's about all."

"It was passion that made me a scientist," said Valentin Gavrilovich Vasilyev. "A passion for new things, a wander-lust. I've trekked and cycled all over our wonderful country. And now I've arrived at the Arctic. And when you stop to think how much of our vast land has still to be traversed, properly explored ... it's a grand feeling. Here's to our bound-less, most beautiful country!" toasted the geographer, and emptied his glass.

We all followed suit.

---

the conviction that there is a complete analogy between the devel-opment of plants on Mars and those on the Earth. He discovered zones of vegetation in the desert expanses on Mars, the reflecting power of which is similar to that of plants which grow in the Central Asian deserts of the U.S.S.R.

Of interest are Tikhov's reports of masses of bloom in certain regions of the Martian deserts in the early spring. In colour and character these zones of bloom on Mars are very similar to the vast desert expanses of Central Asia, which for a short period become covered with an unbroken carpet of red poppies.

Recently Tikhov has put forward interesting suppositions regard-ing vegetation on Venus. As there is more than enough warmth on Venus, the plants there, if they really do exist, should reflect all the thermal part of the solar spectrum, that is to say, they should appear to be red. The discovery made by the Soviet astronomer Barabashev at Pulkovo Observatory, when he found yellow and orange rays through the cloud covering of Venus, made it possible for Tikhov to assume that these rays are probably the reflection of the red vegetation covering Venus.

So far not all scientists share G. A. Tikhov's views. It is the task of the astrobotanical section of the Academy of Sciences of the Kazakh S.S R. to look for further, indisputable proofs of the existence of living vegetation on other planets and, first of all, on Mars.

"And you, what have you to tell us?" asked the captain, addressing Krymov.

Krymov became extremely serious.

"It's very complicated," he began pensively, his hand smoothing his bulging brow, "and it will take a long time to tell."

We all began to persuade him. Natasha was devouring the chief with her eyes. Evidently she, too, knew little of his background.

"All right then, I'll tell you," said Krymov, finally acquiescing. "I was born in an Evenki nomad camp. The Evenki used to be called the Tungus."

Are There Canals on Mars?

It was Schiaparelli, during the first great opposition in 1877, who first discovered these strange formations. To him they appeared as absolutely straight lines forming a network covering the planet. He called them canals, being the first to announce the cautious idea that they were artificial creations of the rational inhabitants of the planet.

Later investigations threw doubts on the existence of these canals. Later observers failed to see them.

The outstanding astronomer Lowell devoted his life to the problem of the existence of life on Mars. He set up a special observatory in the Arizona desert where the transparency of the air favoured observations. He confirmed Schiaparelli's discovery and developed his tentative idea.

Lowell discovered and studied an enormous number of canals. He divided them into main arteries (the most visible were, he asserted, double canals), which ran from the poles through the Equator into the opposite hemisphere, and subsidiary canals which ran from the main and intersecting zones in various directions through the arcs of a great circle; that is to say, by the shortest possible route over the surface of the planet (Mars is a planet with a level relief. It has no mountains or noticeable changes of relief).

Lowell discovered two networks of canals, one linked with the south polar region of melting ice, and the other with a similar

"So you're an Evenk!" exclaimed Natasha.

Krymov nodded.

"I was born in an Evenki tent the very year when in the taiga.... But you've all probably heard about the Tungus meteorite that fell in the taiga?"

"We've heard a little. But tell us more about it, it's all very interesting," begged Nizovsky.

"It was an extraordinary occurrence," Krymov went on, animatedly. "Thousands of people saw a fiery ball, brighter than the sun, above the taiga. A fiery column pierced the cloudless sky. Then followed a shock, the force of which cannot be compared with anything known. It reverberated throughout the entire globe. It was heard more than a thou-

---

northern region. Each of these networks became visible in turn. When the northern ice was melting the canals could be noticed running from the northern ice; when the southern ice was melting, the field of vision showed canals running from the southern ice.

All this enabled Lowell to maintain that the canals were an immense irrigation network of the Martians, who had constructed a gigantic system for utilising the waters formed by the melting of the polar ice-caps. Lowell calculated that the power of the water-pumping system of Mars must be 4,000 times greater than the power of the Niagara Falls. Lowell saw confirmation of his idea in the fact that the canals appear gradually, from the moment the ice begins to melt. They lengthen, it seemed, as the water passes down them. It was established that the lengthening canal (or the water in it) covers a distance across Mars of 4,250 kilometres in the course of 52 days, which is 3.4 kilometres an hour.

Lowell also established that at the points of intersection of the canals there are patches which he calls oases. He is prepared to consider that these oases are the large centres of the inhabitants of Mars, their towns.

However, Lowell's idea was not generally accepted. The very existence of the canals was doubted. When Mars was examined through more powerful telescopes, no canals in the form of unbroken, straight formations were discovered. Only isolated collections

sand kilometres from the place of the catastrophe; it is on record that a train was stopped near Kansk nearly eight hundred kilometres away. The engine-driver testified that it seemed to him that something exploded in his train. An unprecedented hurricane swept the earth. Roofs were blown off and fences fell down four hundred kilometres from where the explosion had occurred. Still farther away kitchen utensils shook and clocks stopped, as happens during earthquakes. The shock was registered at several seismological stations: in Tashkent, in Jena (Germany), and in Irkutsk where eyewitness accounts were collected."

---

of spots were observed, which the eye deliberately endeavoured to join into straight lines.

The canals began to be ascribed to an optical illusion which only a few investigators were able to observe.

However, an objective method of investigation was of assistance.

Working at the Pulkovo Observatory, G. A. Tikhov became the first scientist in the world to photograph the canals on Mars. A photographic plate is not an eye, it would seem that it should not be able to make a mistake.

In recent years the photographing of the canals has been proceeding on an increasingly large scale.

Thus, during the 1924 opposition, Tremiler obtained more than a thousand Martian canal photographs. Further photographs confirmed their existence.

Of extreme interest was the investigation into the colour of the mysterious canals. In every respect their colour resembles the changing colour of the zone of continuous vegetation on Mars.

A calculation of the width of the canals (from 100 to 600 kilometres) led to the idea that they are not "canals or open cuttings in the soil, filled with water," but were rather strips of vegetation which appeared gradually as the water of the melting ice flowed along huge water-carrying pipes (at a speed of 3.4 kilometres an hour. With the same speed there followed in the course of time a wave of vegetation growth). These strips of vegetation (forests or

"What was it, actually?" asked Nizovsky. "The shock from a meteorite hitting the earth?"

"That's what was thought at the time," replied Krymov, evasively. "The air wave went twice round the globe. It was registered by barographs in London and other places.

"Strange phenomena were observed throughout the world for four days and nights after the catastrophe in the taiga. High in the sky luminescent clouds were observed which made the nights throughout Europe and even in Algiers so light that it was possible to read the newspapers at midnight, just as during the white nights at Leningrad."

"When was this?" asked the captain.

---

fields) change their colour in accordance with changes in the seasons of the year.

The assumption that there exist waterpipes buried in the ground with vents in the form of wells might reconcile the observers who had seen the canals and those others who had not seen the straight lines, but only separate dots situated in straight lines. These dots resembled the oases of artificially irrigated vegetation in the places where the water pipes were brought to the surface.

The idea that there exist buried pipes is all the more natural since, in the conditions of small atmospheric pressure on Mars, any open reservoir would result in rapid loss of water through intense evaporation.

The dispute about the nature of the canals still continues, but doubt is no longer thrown on their actual existence.

Avoiding the overbold assumption of irrigation works constructed by rational inhabitants on Mars, some scientists prefer to regard the "canals" as fissures of volcanic origin which, incidentally, have not been found on any other planet in the solar system. This hypothesis has the defect that it cannot explain the movement of water along the canals without the existence of some powerful water-pumping system that passes the polar water across the equator to the opposite hemisphere.

Another view that some astronomers are inclined to hold is that the coloured, geometrically exact, strips on Mars, which change

"The year I was born," replied Krymov, "in 1908. A fiery hurricane swept through the taiga then. In the Vanovar factory, sixty kilometres away, people lost consciousness, feeling that their outer clothing was on fire. The air wave threw numerous reindeer into the air, and as for the trees of the taiga... Believe me, I come from those parts and spent many years joining in the search for the meteorite. All the trees in a radius of thirty kilometres were uprooted, every single one of them! In a radius of sixty kilometres they were overthrown on all the elevated places.

"The hurricane caused unprecedented devastation. The Evenki rushed to the stricken taiga to search for their rein-

---

in length and colour, are traces of the life work of some living beings who have achieved their highest level of mental development which was no less than that of the people on the Earth.

What Were the Circumstances of the 1908 Tungus Catastrophe?

On the basis of testimony from over one thousand eyewitnesses—correspondents of the Irkutsk seismological station and the Irkutsk Observatory, the following has been established:

Early in the morning of June 30, 1908, a fiery body (of the nature of a bolide) hurled through the firmament, leaving behind what looked like a falling meteorite.

At 7 a. m. local time a blinding ball of light which seemed brighter than the sun appeared over the taiga near the Vanovar factory. It became transformed into a fiery column rising up into the cloudless sky.

Nothing of the kind had been seen before when meteorites fell. Nor had there been any such phenomenon when, a few years earlier, a gigantic falling meteorite disintegrated in the air in the Far East.

After the light phenomena, a loud report was heard which reverberated several times like a clap of thunder being transformed into repeated peals. The sound was heard one thousand kilometres distant from the scene of the catastrophe.

deer, corn stores and property. All they found was charred carcases. Misfortune struck the tent of my grandfather Luchetkan as well. My father, who went into the devastated taiga, found there a tremendous column of water spurting from the ground. Some days later my father died in terrible torment, as though suffering from burns.... Yet there was no sign of burns on his skin. The old folk were terrified. They forbade the Evenki to go into the stricken taiga. They called it an accursed place. The shamans said that the god of fire and thunder, Ogdy, had descended to earth there. It was said that he would burn with invisible fire everyone who went there.

A hurricane of terrific force followed the noise, tore roofs from houses and uprooted fences over a distance of hundreds of kilo-metres.

Houses suffered the sort of damage characteristic of earthquakes. Earth tremors were registered by many seismological stations: in Irkutsk, Tashkent and Jena (Germany). Two tremors were regis-tered at Irkutsk (close to the scene of the catastrophe). The second was weaker and, so the director of the station affirmed, was caused by a blast which reached Irkutsk after some delay.

The blast was also registered in London and twice circled the globe.

For three days after the catastrophe, luminescent clouds were observed at an altitude of 86 kilometres over the territory of Europe and North Africa, and by their light photographs could be taken and newspapers read during the night-time.

Academician A. A. Polkanov, who was in Siberia at the time, was a man of great gifts in the observation and registration of what he saw. He wrote in his diary: "The sky is covered with a dense layer of clouds, it is pouring with rain yet, at the same time, it is extraordinarily light. In fact it is so light that out of doors one can read small newspaper type fairly easily. There should be no moon, yet the clouds are illuminated by a sort of yellowish-green light which sometimes changes to pink." If the mysterious nocturnal light which Academician Polkanov observed was reflected solar

"In the beginning of the nineteen-twenties," continued Krymov, "Kulik, a Russian scientist, arrived at the Vanovar factory. He wanted to find the meteorite. The Evenki refused to accompany him. He did hire two Angara hunters, and I joined them. I was young and knew Russian well, I had learned a little in the factory and feared nothing on earth.

"With Kulik we arrived at the centre of the catastrophe. We discovered that all the countless trees, the millions of overthrown tree trunks, were lying with their roots pointing in the direction of one spot, the centre of the catastrophe. When we examined the centre itself, we were astounded. For there where the destruction caused by a fallen meteorite should have been greatest, the forest stood upright. It was

---

light, it would have been white and not yellowish-green and pink.

Twenty years later, in Soviet times, Kulik's expedition went to the scene of the catastrophe. An exact account of the results of many years of search by the expedition is given by the astronomer in our story.

The assumption that it was a huge meteorite that fell in the Tungus taiga, although the one more usually made, still does not explain the following points:

a) the absence of any meteorite fragments,

b) the absence of any crater or hollows,

c) the existence of standing trees at the centre of the catastrophe,

d) the presence of underground waters under pressure, after the meteorite had fallen,

e) the spout of water which gushed up during the first days after the catastrophe,

f) the appearance of a blinding ball like the sun at the time of the catastrophe,

g) the accidents to the Evenki who visited the scene of the catastrophe immediately after it had occurred.

The external picture of the explosion in the Tungus taiga fully coincides with the picture of an atomic explosion.

The assumption that such an explosion did take place in the air over the taiga would explain all the circumstances as follows:

inexplicable not only to me, but even to the Russian scientist I could see as much from the expression on his face.

"The trees were standing upright, but they were dead trees—no twigs, no tops, looking like poles driven into the earth.

"In the middle of the forest of trees there was water—a lake or swamp.

"Kulik assumed that this was the hole made by the fallen meteorite.

"Simply and kindly he explained to us hunters, just as though we were his scientific assistants, that somewhere in the Arizona desert in America there is a huge crater about a mile in diameter and about 600 feet deep. It was formed

---

The trees in the centre were standing upright since the blast hit them from above, lopping off branches and tree-tops.

The luminescent clouds were the effect on the air of the remains of radioactive substances which were carried upwards.

The accidents in the taiga were the result of radioactive particles falling into the soil.

The sublimation, conversion into vapour, of an entire body hurtling into the Earth's atmosphere is natural at the temperature of an atomic explosion (20 million degrees Centigrade) and, of course, it was hardly possible to find anything left after it.

The spout of water which gushed up immediately after the catastrophe was caused by the formation of fissures in the stratum of frozen rock as a result of the blast.

Is It Possible for a Radioactive Meteorite to Explode?

No, it is not possible. The substances of which meteorites are formed are the same as those found on the Earth. The amount, say, of uranium in meteorites is about a two hundred thousand millionth of one per cent. For a chain reaction with atomic fall-out to be possible it would require a uranium meteorite in the pure form and, moreover, in the form also of the most rare isotope Uranium-235. This has never been found in the pure form.

thousands of years ago by the falling of a gigantic heavenly body, a meteorite, like that which had fallen here and which it was essential to find. From then on I was consumed with a desire to help the Russian professor.

"The following year Kulik returned to the taiga with a large expedition. He hired workmen. Of course, I was the first to join him. We searched for pieces of the meteorite. We dried out the central swamp in the dead forest, investigated all the hollows, but we not only found no trace of the meteorite, but none of any crater left by it either.

"For ten years Kulik returned each year to the taiga; for

Besides this, even if we imagine such an unlikely case as there being such a piece of "refined" Uranium-235 in the natural state, it could never really exist because Uranium-235 undergoes spontaneous disintegration through the accidental explosion of some of its atoms. With the first accidental explosion of this kind, the whole imaginary meteorite would explode immediately it was formed.

If an atomic explosion is to be assumed, then it is inevitable to assume also that the explosion was due to some radioactive substance obtained by artificial means.

Where Could a Space-ship Using Radioactive Fuel Have Come from?

The nearest star to us that is presumed to have a planetary system round it is in the constellation of Cygnus. The Pulkovo astronomer Deich first discovered it. It is nine light years distant from the Earth. To cover this distance one would require to fly at the speed of light for nine whole years! Of course, no space-ship could possibly attain such a speed One can only speak of the degree of approximation to it. We know that the elementary particles of matter—electrons—move at a speed of up to 300 thousand kilometres a second. If we assume that, as the result of prolonged impulse, a space-ship could attain such a speed, we should find that it would take several decades to cover the distance from our planet to the star nearest to us. But this is where Einstein's paradox comes to

ten years I accompanied him in his fruitless search. The meteorite had vanished.

"Kulik assumed that it had fallen into the swamp and that the swamp had swallowed up the crater. But we drilled through the soil and came up against an undamaged stratum of eternally frozen rock. After drilling, a jet of water burst through the bore-hole. If the meteorite had penetrated and melted this frozen stratum, it could not have been restored. Even in the winter the earth does not now freeze below about six feet.

"After the second year of the expedition's work I went with Kulik to Moscow and began to study there. But every sum-

---

our aid. For people flying at a speed approximating to that of light, time would pass more slowly, much more slowly than for those observing their flight; after being in flight for decades they would discover that life on the Earth had passed through millennia. . . .

It is difficult to speak of time in connection with beings unknown to us, but if we imagine such a flight from the Earth the travellers setting out would have to spend the whole of their lives; until they were very aged, on it. This is quite apart from any consideration of more distant stars and their planets.

Far more real would be the assumption that a flight was made from a nearer planet, in the first place from Mars.

What Is the Evidence of Astronautics?

Mars moves round the Sun in an ellipse making one revolution in 687 terrestrial days (1.8808 terrestrial years).

The orbits of the Earth and Mars approach each other at a point where the Earth passes in the summer. Every two years the Earth meets Mars at this place, but they are particularly close to each other only once in 15-17 years. The distance between the planets is then reduced from 400 million to 55 million kilometres (the great opposition).

It is not to be supposed, however, that it is enough for a spaceship to cover only this distance.

mer I returned to search for the meteorite near my native home. Kulik's efforts continued. I always accompanied him. I was no longer a semi-literate hunter from the taiga. I was a university student, I had read a great deal and had even begun to contribute my own criticism in the scientific field. But I said nothing of this to Kulik. I knew with what iron will, with what passionate certainty he was searching for his meteorite; he had even dedicated some verses to it. . . . How could I tell him that I had come to the conviction that there had never been a meteorite?"

"What d'you mean, there had never been one?" exclaimed Nizovsky. "What about the marks of the catastrophe and the stricken trees?"

Each planet moves in its own orbit: the Earth at a speed of 30 kilometres a second, Mars at 24 kilometres a second.

On leaving the planet, a rocket space-ship has the Earth's speed along the orbit in a direction perpendicular to the shortest route between the planets. To make the space-ship fly in a straight line, the lateral speed along the orbit would have to be abolished, which would require the useless expenditure of tremendous energy. It is more advantageous to fly along a curve using the speed along the orbit and adding to the space-ship only the speed necessary for it to break away from the planet.

It requires a speed of 5.1 kilometres a second to make the break-away from Mars, and 11.3 kilometres a second to make the break-away from the Earth.

Sternfeld, a prominent Soviet astronautical expert, has made an accurate calculation of the navigational routes and times of flight for a space-ship, as applicable to the oppositions of 1907 and 1909. His results indicate that a space-ship from Mars, using the greatest economy of fuel and having left Mars at the most suitable time, should have reached the Earth either in 1907 or 1909, but on no account in 1908! However, with a flight from Venus, utilising the opposition of the Earth and Venus in 1908, the astronauts should have arrived on the earth on June 30, 1908!

"There was a catastrophe all right, but not a meteorite," said Krymov impressively. "I've thought a lot about how the trees could have remained standing at the centre of the catastrophe. What causes the explosion when a meteorite drops? The meteorite flies into the earth's atmosphere at a cosmic speed of 30-60 kilometres a second. With its great mass and gigantic speed, the meteorite has tremendous kinetic energy. When it is brought to a standstill by hitting the earth all this energy has to pass into heat; it's this that causes the terrifically powerful explosion. But in our case, this didn't happen. There was no encounter between the meteorite and the earth. To me it was obvious. The existence of the dead timber led me to think that the explosion had occurred in the air, at a

---

This is an absolutely perfect coincidence which makes far-reaching assumptions possible.

According to this, just before the great opposition of 1909, the Martians, after reaching the Earth in 1908, would have found that they had the most advantageous conditions for returning to Mars.

Were Any Signals Given from Mars?

An article entitled "Mars and Its Canals" published in the collection *New Ideas in Astronomy,* which appeared soon after the great opposition of 1909, speaks of light signals from Mars observed in 1909.

The sensational talk at the time about radio-signals being received from Mars at the beginning of the twenties of this century during the opposition of the Earth and Mars is universally known.

Those were the days of the first expansion of radio-engineering, which had been founded by the brilliant scientist Popov, and of the first appearance of universally procurable wireless sets.

Y. Perelman writes in the supplement to his book *Inter-planetary Travel* that when Mars was close to the Earth in 1920 and 1922, the Earth's wireless sets were receiving signals which by their nature could not have been sent out by the Earth's radio-stations

height of approximately three hundred metres, and exactly over these trees."

"How, in the air?" remarked Nizovsky incredulously.

"The explosive wave went in all directions," Krymov continued confidently. "Where the trees were perpendicular to its front, that is, directly under the explosion, the wave did not fell the trees, it simply lopped off all the branches and broke the tree-tops. Where its blow came at an angle, all the trees in a radius of thirty to sixty kilometres were overthrown. The explosion could only have occurred up in the air!"

"Indeed, that seems as if it could be the truth," said Nizovsky, pensively rubbing his chin.

(having in mind primarily the wave-length, which was extremely limited for the Earth's transmitting stations of those days). So the signals were ascribed to Mars.

Marconi and his engineers, who had a taste for sensations, set out on special expeditions to the Andes and the Atlantic Ocean to pick up signals from Mars. Marconi tried to do so on a 300,000 metre wave.

The Explosion on Mars

After the great opposition of the Earth and Mars in 1956, A. A. Mikhailov, Director of Pulkovo Observatory and Corresponding Member of the U.S.S.R. Academy of Sciences, reported to a gathering of scientists at the Leningrad Scientists' Club in Lesnoye, that the Pulkovo Observatory had registered an explosion of tremendous force on Mars. Judging by the fact that the consequences of the explosion had actually been observed through telescopes, and knowing that no volcanoes exist on Mars, the explosion had to be attributed to a nuclear explosion rather than to anything else. It is difficult to imagine a nuclear explosion on Mars that was not deliberately caused. It is very likely that the explosion was made for some constructional purpose. Thus, the Pulkovo Observatory observations can serve as one of the proofs in favour of the existence of rational life on Mars.

"But what sort of explosion could have occurred in the air?" argued the astronomer aloud. "For there was no conversion of the kinetic energy into heat, nor could there have been. That problem worried me."

"At the university we had an inter-planetary communications group. I was very interested in Tsiolkovsky and his inter-planetary rocket with its reserves of liquid oxygen and hydrogen. One day an idea struck me—it was a very bold idea. If Kulik had been with me I would immediately have told him about it, but... the war came. In spite of his age, Leonid Alexeyevich Kulik volunteered for the front and was killed in action."

What Is the History of the Hypothesis?

The first hypothesis about the atomic explosion of a space-ship in the Tungus taiga in 1908 was referred to in A. Kazantsev's story "Explosion" (see *Vokrug Sveta, Round the World*, 1946).

On February 20, 1948, the author expounded his hypothesis at a meeting of the All-Union Astronomical Society in the Moscow Planetarium.

The Moscow Planetarium popularized this hypothesis in its showing of "The Riddle of the Tungus Meteorite."

Later in 1948 a letter published in No. 9 of the magazine *Tekhnika Molodyozhi (Technique for the Youth)*, by some important astronomers defended the plausibility of the hypothesis of a space rocket explosion in the Tungus taiga. Among the scientists subscribing to it were: Professor A. A. Mikhailov, Director of Pulkovo Observatory and Corresponding Member of the U.S.S.R. Academy of Sciences; Professor P. P. Parenago, President of the Moscow Branch of the All-Union Astronomical Society; Professor B. A. Vorontsov-Velyaminov, Corresponding Member of the Academy of Pedagogical Sciences; Professor K. L. Bayev, Professor M. Y. Nabokov, and others.

Subsequently, Professor A. A. Mikhailov proposed his own version of the Tungus catastrophe. He suggested that the Tungus meteorite was a comet, but this suggestion was not widely echoed.

For a moment Krymov was silent; then he continued:

"I was on a different sector of the front. I often watched big shells exploding in the air. And I became more and more convinced that the explosion in the taiga had indeed taken place in the air. And the explosion could only have been the explosion of fuel in a space-ship trying to descend to the Earth."

"A space-ship from some other planet?" Nizovsky was almost shouting, as he leapt from his chair.

The geographer leaned back in his chair. The captain grunted and emptied his glass of brandy. Natasha sat goggling at Krymov as though seeing him for the first time.

One of Kulik's assistants, V. A. Sytin, considered that it was not a falling meteorite, but a mighty whirlwind that caused the Tungus catastrophe. But this does not explain the appearance of the catastrophe site and many other details.

Academician Fesenkov, as well as Krinov, Scientific Secretary of the Meteorite Committee of the U.S.S.R. Academy of Sciences, Professor Stanyukovich, Astapovich and other meteorite experts consistently adhered to the view that actually a meteorite weighing about a million tons had fallen in the Tungus taiga. They firmly rejected every other view of the matter.

Aerodynamical Investigations

Very many people were interested in this problem of the Tungus meteorite. A. Y. Monotskov, the designer of excellent Soviet gliders and well known as the aerodynamics expert and aircraft designer of the Antonov group, approached the problem in strictly scientific manner. He made an analysis of the testimony of the vast number of eyewitnesses, correspondents of the Irkutsk Observatory, and then attempted to determine the speed at which the supposed "meteorite" had passed over various districts. He made a map showing the trajectory of the flight and the time at which the meteorite had been spotted by eyewitnesses at different points of the trajectory. Monotskov's map led to the unexpected conclusion that the "me-

"Yes, a visitor from outer space, a space-ship from another planet, most likely from Mars. It is only on Mars that one can assume that life exists. I thought at that time that the reserves of liquid hydrogen and oxygen—the only type of fuel suitable for cosmic flights—had exploded. That's what I thought before...."

"What? You mean that's not what you think now?" exclaimed Natasha. There was obvious disappointment in her tone. Evidently the idea of a visitor from outer space had been just what she wanted.

"Yes, I think differently now," Krymov said calmly. "The

---

teorite" had slowed down as it flew over the earth. Monotskov calculated the speed of the "meteorite" when it was over the scene of the explosion and the answer he obtained was 0.7 kilometres a second (and not 30-60 kilometres a second, as had been thought previously!). In fact, the speed approximated to the speed of a modern jet plane and is an argument of no little importance in favour of the conclusion that the "Tungus meteorite" was, as Monotskov believes, some kind of "flying apparatus"—an inter-planetary space-ship. If a meteorite had fallen at such a speed then, on the basis of conclusions drawn from aerodynamics, it follows that to cause the devastation in the taiga it would have had to have a mass not of a million tons, as the astronomers had calculated, but of a thousand million tons, and a diameter of one kilometre. This does not correspond to the observations made, for the flying meteorite did not obscure the sky. Clearly the energy causing the destruction in the taiga was not heat energy but, more likely, nuclear energy released by an atomic explosion of the space-ship's fuel, the space-ship not striking the earth.

Is the Dispute Scientific or Unscientific?

Those who support the hypothesis of a falling meteorite have repeatedly opposed the hypothesis of the explosion of a space-ship from some other planet occurring in the Tungus taiga. Their arguments are as follows:

135

atomic explosions in Japan convinced me about the kind of fuel that was on the space-ship.

"After the war ended I devoted myself to the problem of Mars. I had to prove the existence of life on that planet. I began to study under Tikhov. And now here I am with the expedition that is to make a study of the absorption of heat rays by arctic plants."

"And what will that prove?" The words came from the captain.

"As far back as last century Timiryazev proposed trying to discover chlorophyll on Mars. That would have proved that the green patches on Mars, which change colour according to

---

1) To deny that it was a falling meteorite is unscientific (why?).

2) A meteorite did fall, but was swallowed up in the swamp.

3) A crater was formed, but the swampy soil caused it to be covered over.

Academicians Fesenkov and Krinov advanced these arguments in an article "Meteorite or Martian Space-ship?" published in *Literaturnaya Gazeta* in August 1951.

The publication of the article had an effect exactly contrary to what its writers wished. Immediately millions of readers learned of the hypothesis of a Martian space-ship. The newspaper received large numbers of letters. Some of these pointed out with some justification that:

a) If a meteorite really fell and was swallowed up in the swamp where is it now? Why has it not been discovered in the depths by means of magnetic instruments? Why were not pieces of it scattered about, as always happens when meteorites fall?

b) If a crater had been formed, it should have been not smaller than that of the Arizona meteorite, namely 1.5 kilometres in diameter and up to 180 metres deep; and if this crater, as meteorite experts assert, disappeared under the swampy soil, then why was there no trace in the centre of the catastrophe of any crater formation, and still more, why did the stratum of peat there, and also *the stratum of eternal frost, remain intact? The latter should have been melted.* What caused the "swampy soil which covered the crathe seasons of the year just as vegetation changes colour on the earth, are areas covered with vegetation."

"Well, was chlorophyll discovered?"

"No, there was no such luck. There is no absorption band of the spectrum characteristic of chlorophyll to be found on Mars. Moreover, when the green patches on Mars are photographed in infra-red rays, they do not appear white, as with vegetation on the earth. Everything seemed to point to there being no vegetation on Mars at all. But Gavriil Andrianovich Tikhov offered a marvellous suggestion. Why does the vegetation of the Earth appear white in such photographs? Because it reflects the heat rays it does not need. But on Mars

---

ter" to become frozen again, as though the ice age had once more returned to the Earth?

As is known, the meteorite experts gave no replies to these questions, nor could they do so.

The Sensational Solution of the Riddle of the Tungus Meteorite

Years passed and no visitors returned to the place where the supposed meteorite had fallen in the Tungus taiga. However, interest in it remained strong, perhaps because of the outer space hypothesis connected with it. And in 1957 meteorite experts were compelled to refer to the question again in the press. Krinov in *Komsomolskaya Pravda* and Professor Stanyukovich in the magazine *In Defence of Peace* made the sensational announcement that the riddle of the Tungus meteorite had at last been solved! There had indeed been a meteorite, only ... it had disintegrated in the air. So at long last the meteorite experts had given up asserting that some heavenly body had struck the Earth but that the crater had been "lost"! But no! Even this logical argument was unacceptable. All that the meteorite experts were interested in was that part of the meteorite had disintegrated in the air. As proof, it was reported that some old tins containing soil had been found in the cellars of the Academy of Sciences, and that at one time they had been brought from the scene of the Tungus catastrophe. An analysis of

the sun does not shine brightly. There the vegetation has to try to use all the possible heat. Might not that be the reason why the green patches did not become white in infra-red rays?

"Strictly speaking, this is the reason why we astronomers are in the Arctic. We want to verify whether the arctic vegetation reflects heat rays."

"Well, does it?" we all asked in chorus.

"No, it doesn't! Northern plants absorb it, just like the plants on Mars," shouted Natasha. Her eyes were shining. "We can prove that life on Mars does exist, that the green patches are vast coniferous forests! That the famous canals on Mars are strips of vegetation from 100 to 600 kilometres wide!"

---

these abandoned tins revealed particles of metallic dust, a fraction of a millimetre in dimension, in the soil. Chemical analysis established the presence of iron, 7 per cent of nickel and about 0.7 per cent of cobalt and also small magnetic spherules one-hundredth part of a millimetre in size, the product of melting metal in air. But the hasty announcement that the riddle of the Tungus catastrophe was now solved turned out to be a little premature.

Indeed, if the meteorite experts become compelled to agree that the meteorite did not strike the Earth, but that for some unknown reason it was transformed into dust, then it is reasonable to ask the question: why was it transformed into dust? What caused *the explosion in the Tungus taiga,* if no heavenly body struck the Earth and the kinetic energy of the meteorite was not transformed into heat energy? And, if the meteorite did not disintegrate, what was the origin of the collossal energy that overthrew trees over an area of hundreds of square kilometres in the taiga? To all these perfectly natural questions the meteorite experts, who stubbornly cling to the meteorite version of the catastrophe, *offer no reply, nor can there be any.*

Incidentally, the metal dust found in the samples of soil from the Tungus taiga does not in any way prove that it is without doubt the remains of the meteorite. The iron structure which is characteristic of meteorites was not found. Most likely it is part of the

"Now just a minute, Natasha," said the astronomer, interrupting his assistant.

"Canals?" repeated Nizovsky. "Then they do exist. But not so long ago people were saying it was all an optical illusion."

"The canals on Mars have been photographed and photographs don't lie. More than a thousand of them have been photographed. They have been studied. It has been proved that they appear and gradually lengthen from the poles to the equator as the polar ice on Mars melts."

"The strips of vegetation lengthen at a speed of three and a half kilometres an hour," interjected Natasha who was quite unable to keep silent.

---

remains of the bodywork of an inter-planetary rocket destroyed by explosion. The chemical composition of the remains fits the case.

As we see, it is very difficult to sweep aside the explanation that the Tungus catastrophe was an atomic explosion. The inquiring mind is not to be convinced by references to science honours degrees which, at the same time, disregard the indubitable fact of an explosion of tremendous force in the Tungus taiga. The inquiring mind is anxious for scientists to produce the true explanation for the riddle of the Tungus meteorite.

How Can We Find the Solution to the Riddle?

The findings of an expedition to the Tungus taiga would be of great interest.

The question as to whether or not an atomic explosion did take place in the Tungus taiga can be solved. All it requires is an investigation in the locality where the catastrophe occurred, an investigation of radioactivity there.

A definite norm of radioactivity exists for ordinary places on the Earth. With Geiger counters it is possible in any spot to discover a definite amount of atomic fall-out.

If, when the explosion occurred, there was powerful radioactive radiation (an atomic explosion) in the area of the catastrophe, then an avalanche of neutrons (elementary particles which fall out when

"At the same speed as a current of water in a whirlpool?" queried the astounded geographer.

"Yes, at that very same speed," confirmed the astronomer. "It seems amazing that this whole network of strips of vegetation consists of ideally straight lines, the chief of which, like arteries, run from the melting polar ice to the equator."

"Without doubt, then, this is a vast irrigation network created by the Martians for irrigating the fields, and we have taken them for canals. But there are no canals, of course. There are pipes laid down on the earth," suggested Nizovsky, carried away by the subject.

Krymov corrected him with a smile.

"Laid down on Mars, not on the Earth."

"Then there is life on Mars! Then, you're right," continued Nizovsky.

"All we can say with certainty so far is that life on Mars is not impossible."

"For all we know the Martians really could have flown to the Earth in 1908," said the captain.

"Yes, they could," replied Krymov, unperturbed.

---

atoms break up), passing through the timber of the trees and the soil, would inevitably have caused certain changes. There should have appeared what are known as "labelled atoms," with heavier nuclei, in which some of the flying neutrons were caught. These labelled atoms are heavier isotopes (varieties) of the elements usually encountered on the Earth. Thus, for example, ordinary nitrogen could be transformed into heavy carbon, undergoing slow spontaneous disintegration. Other heavy isotopes disintegrate in the same way. This spontaneous destruction can be detected with the aid of the same Geiger counters.

If it becomes possible to establish in the area of the Tungus taiga that the disintegration of atoms per second is in excess of the normal, then the nature of the Tungus taiga catastrophe will be obvious. It will then also be possible to ascertain the locality of the centre of the catastrophe and, if it coincides with the dead trees, to re-establish the complete picture of the loss of the Martian space-ship.

"Martians on Earth of all things!" muttered Boris Yefimovich, pulling on his pipe.

"Mars is a planet of dying life. As it is smaller in size and has a smaller force of gravitation than the Earth, Mars could not retain the original atmosphere. Its particles broke away from the planet and flew into outer space. The air on Mars became rarefied, the oceans began to evaporate and the air vapour vanished in the depths of outer space. So little water remained on Mars that it could be contained in our Baikal alone."

"Then they flew out in order to seize our Earth," decided Nizovsky. "They wanted our flourishing planet!"

"As if we hadn't enough Hitlers, Trumans and MacArthurs," growled the captain. "Now we have to cope also with Martians!"

"I think you're wrong. Wells and other Western writers, when they imagine the worlds coming together, can only think in terms of invasions and wars. To my mind, knowing the state of things as regards water on Mars, and seeing the vast irrigation works of the Martians, we can draw certain conclusions about their social system which promotes the carrying out of planned economy on the scale of the entire planet."

"You mean they have some sort of perfect social system there?" asked Nizovsky.

"The development of the social life of rational beings can lead to nothing else," said the geographer with conviction.

"Undoubtedly," confirmed Krymov. "But water is disappearing from Mars all the time. Its inhabitants have to see to it that life continues to be possible for future generations, just as our contemporaries are attending to the life of future generations here. The Martians must get water for Mars. Water exists! It exists on the planets closest to Mars and in abundance, primarily, on the Earth. Take Greenland. It is covered with a layer of ice three kilometres thick. If it were removed, the climate of Europe would be considerably improved. Oranges would grow in the countryside round Moscow. And if the ice were carried to Mars it would melt there and cover the entire planet with a layer 50 metres deep; it would practically fill up the hollows of former oceans and the planet would come to life again for many millions of years!"

"Then the Martians only want the Earth's water, and not the Earth itself?" asked Nizovsky.

"Of course. Living conditions on the Earth are so different from those on Mars that the Martians could not breathe or move about freely on our Earth; they would weigh twice as much here. Just imagine being double your weight. The Martians have no reason to conquer the Earth. What's more, as they have reached a high level of culture and have a perfect social system, they probably only know about wars from their own historical researches. They would come to us here as friends, for help, for ice."

"The friendship of the planets!" ejaculated Nizovsky. "But how can Greenland's ice be transferred to Mars?"

"If a metal space-ship can make the inter-planetary journey, then a space-ship made of ice or filled with ice could do the same journey. Millions of such space-ships sent from the Earth to Mars, not all at once of course, perhaps over a period of centuries, would finally transfer the whole of Greenland's ice to Mars, which in the interim would be adapting itself to new conditions that would be better than before. Atomic energy will give the space-ship the power it needs."

"Atomic energy!" said the geographer. "Then you are convinced it was atomic fuel that blew up in the Tungus taiga?"

"I'm absolutely sure it was. There are many proofs of it. Besides what I have said already, I may add something. Do you remember the luminescent clouds? They gave out more than reflected white sunlight. During the nights a greenish and pinkish light was observed which even penetrated through the clouds. It was undoubtedly caused by the luminescence of the air. The moment the space-ship blew up all the matter was vapourized and rose in the air where the remnants of radioactive substance continued to disintegrate, making the air luminescent. You should remember how Luchetkan's son died, and how there were no burns on his body. That was most certainly a radioactive consequence such as occurs shortly after an atomic explosion."

"All this is extremely like what happened in Nagasaki and Hiroshima," said the geographer.

"But who was flying to us, and why did they die?" asked Natasha.

For a brief moment Krymov was plunged in thought.

"I asked eminent astronauts to calculate for me when would be the most suitable time for the Martians to fly from Mars to the Earth. You see, Mars comes particularly close to the Earth once in fifteen years."

"When did it occur?"

"In 1909!" said Natasha, excitedly.

"Then it doesn't fit," remarked the captain, disappointed.

"If you must know, it does not fit. It suited the Martians to fly to the Earth in 1907 or 1909, but on no account on June 30, 1908."

"What a pity!" sighed Nizovsky.

Krymov smiled.

"Wait a minute. I haven't said everything. The calculation of the astronauts drew attention to a remarkable coincidence."

"Yes, what?"

"If the space-ship had flown from Venus, then the most suitable day for the flight would have been June 30, 1908."

"And when did the catastrophe occur in the taiga?"

"On June 30, 1908."

"Well, I'm blessed!" cried Nizovsky. "Were they inhabitants of Venus, then?"

"I don't think so.... Incidentally, it is interesting that the astronauts point out that the conditions for a flight from Venus to the Earth at that time were astonishingly favourable. The rocket should have set off on May 20, 1908 and, flying in the same direction as Venus and the Earth, keeping between them all the time, should have arrived on the Earth a few days before the opposition of Venus and the Earth."

"Of course, it was inhabitants from Venus! It's indisputable!" said Nizovsky, heatedly.

"I don't think so..." objected the astronomer, stubbornly. "There is too much carbon dioxide on Venus, and there are some indications of poisonous gases there. It is hard to imagine highly-developed animal life on Venus."

"But nevertheless they did fly here. That means they do exist," insisted Nizovsky. "You're not going to say that Martians flew here from Venus."

"You've guessed right. That is just what I imagine."

"Well, I must say!" said Nizovsky, shattered. "What proofs have you?"

"The proofs exist. It is perfectly rational to suppose that in the search for water that could be made use of the Martians decided to investigate both neighbouring planets, Venus and the Earth. At first, at the most suitable time they flew to Venus and then, on May 20, 1908, they flew from Venus to the Earth. Evidently the explorers died en route from the action of cosmic rays, through encountering a meteorite or from some other cause. It was an unguided space-ship, resembling a meteorite in every respect, that was approaching the Earth. That is why it flew into the atmosphere without reducing its speed by braking. Because of air friction on the space-ship it grew hot, like a meteorite does. Its outer covering melted and the atomic fuel was then in conditions where a chain reaction became possible. An atomic explosion occurred in the air. Thus the visitors from outer space died on the very day when their rocket, as precise calculations now show, should have landed on the Earth. It is possible that the day was awaited with alarm on Mars."

"Why do you think so?"

"Because in 1909, during the great opposition, many astronomers on our Earth were agitated by bursts of light observed on Mars."

"Could they have been signals?"

"Yes, some people talked of signals, but their voices were drowned in the objections of the sceptics."

"They were signalling to their space travellers, perhaps?" suggested Natasha.

"Possibly," replied the astronomer. "Fifteen years passed. By that time, by 1924, the radio, discovered by the Russian scientist Popov, already existed. And so, during the opposition many radio-sets received strange signals! Then there was a lot of shouting about radio-signals from Mars. There was talk about it being a joke on the part of Marconi. But he denied it. However, he fell for the sensation stories and even tried himself to pick up signals from Mars; he organised a special expedition, but got nothing. No one could decipher the strange signals received on some wave-length that the Earth's radio-stations do not work on."

"What about the next opposition?" asked Nizovsky excitedly.

"In 1939 nothing was observed, either by astronomers or

radio-experts. The Martians may have been trying to get in touch with their own space travellers during the previous opposition, but possibly they decided later that they'd perished."

"How logical it all sounds, and how very moving!" remarked Nizovsky.

"The next opposition of Mars will be in 1954," said Krymov, after a moment's silence. "I don't know whether the Martians will by then have solved the problem of protecting the organism from the action of cosmic rays in inter-planetary space. . . . I don't know. Personally I have other hopes. We already understand atomic energy. It is we who will be capable in the near future of entertaining the idea of space flights."

"Will you fly to Mars?" asked Natasha, somewhat terrified at the idea.

"Yes, I'm confident I shall fly to Mars. The development of rational beings, the development of science on the Earth is proceeding in immeasurably more favourable conditions than on Mars. We shall fly to it sooner and more successfully than they did. . . ."

Krymov was silent for a moment, then laughed aloud.

"So now you see why I became an astronomer. I think I've told you far more than I intended, thanks to the brandy."

"Just a moment," said Nizovsky, "I'm a palaeontologist. We can restore the image of an animal that once lived on the Earth by examining bits of bones. Can you not imagine to yourself what a rational inhabitant of Mars looks like? You know all the conditions of his existence. Describe to us what a visitor from outer space would look like."

Krymov smiled.

"I've thought about that. If you like, I'll tell you. . . . Incidentally I have read suppositions put forward by one of your colleagues, Professor Yefremov, the palaeontologist and writer'. I agree with much of what he has written.... A single brain centre and, close to it, organs of stereoscopic sight and hearing.... All that is essential. Then, of course, the Martian must have an upright position to give the broadest view of the locality. As for outward appearance, the climate is severe on Mars, there are sharp temperature changes. The Martians are probably not very handsome. They must have some sort of protective covering, a thick layer of fat, thick fur or skin of a violet colour which, like the Martian vegetation, absorbs heat rays. Martians cannot be very tall ... the force of gravity is not great there ... their muscles must be less developed than ours.... What else, now? Ah, yes! The respiratory organs. Theirs must be most highly-developed, for they have to make use of the insignificant amount of oxygen available in the Martian atmosphere. Actually I can't answer for the accuracy of all this."

"And what would be the appearance of rational beings living on Venus?" asked Nizovsky, thoughtfully.

The astronomer guffawed.

"I've nothing to say on that score, we still know so little."

"Yet they flew from Venus," said Nizovsky softly.

Krymov shook his head.

It was long past midnight when we separated. Boris Yefimovich was delighted with the evening's entertainment.

"What a man! How single-minded he is! We could do with someone like him, in the Arctic!"

I remember when the time came to say good-bye to the astronomer. With Natasha, he landed on Kholodnaya Zemlya in order there, too, to investigate the reflecting properties of the local vegetation.

His apparatus was lowered into the motor launch. Natasha and Krymov turned to wave to us. The captain gave a farewell blast from the ship's siren; he always did that, he was punctilious, was Boris Yefimovich!

Nizovsky leaned over the railings and shouted:

"They came from Venus!"

"No, from Mars!" shouted Krymov in reply, this without a smile on his face, for he was quite serious.

The launch grew smaller and smaller as it sprang through the waves, approaching the jagged line of land in the distance.

An hour later the ship's launch returned.

The *Georgy Sedov* began preparations to resume its course.

ALEXANDER KAZANTSEV
THE MARTIAN

The spectre of the "Martian catastrophe" haunted the saloon of the *Georgy Sedov*. No one now had any desire to talk about Arctic adventures; sailors and polar explorers alike were recalling the details of the Tungus explosion; they became excited and heated arguments arose.... Our "Northern Decameron," as the captain called it, had run aground....

"You'll have to extricate us, Alexander Petrovich," he said, addressing me with a smile. "Let our writer of fantasies relate something fantastic, now that our astronomical guest has put us in the mood."

"Yes, do!" came a chorus of voices from the company assembled in the saloon. "Tell us a story we can't possibly believe!"

"But did you really believe in the space-ship over the taiga?" I asked jocularly.

"The Americans have a saying: in God we trust and the rest in cash," replied the captain. "In my opinion there was a lot of hard cash."

"So much that ... it can't be refuted," put in the air pilot. He was a huge, taciturn fellow, who always went about in his flying-suit and fur boots. It was his job to select the site for an aerodrome on one of the islands, which explained how he came to be a passenger on the *Georgy Sedov*.

"It's not credible, yet it can't be refuted," mused Netayev, the helmsman.

"So I'm to tell you a story you can't possibly believe," I began. I had already decided to sandwich somewhere between the simple tales of Arctic life usually heard in the saloon, some story about a totally different, incredible, perfectly impossible sort of life, but. . . .

They began to listen, perhaps a little incredulously, with condescending or encouraging grins, rather like those of the reader of my story as he turns over this page in anticipation of the fantastic.

The story concerns the present day, a single encounter in a rather uninteresting room with a ceiling that leaks and ink stains on the desks, in the Chkalov Central Air Club at Tushino, outside Moscow.

It was my turn on duty at the club. Don't look so surprised; I'm no pilot. It's simply this: A few years ago we astronautics enthusiasts organized our own astronautics section. It was an organization set up to help promote space flights in the future. Not so very long ago we were ridiculed and jokingly referred to as lunatics, because we dreamed of flying to the moon. But we put up with all that and set to work to make our great idea widely known. We got together all those whom we had managed to inspire with our own faith in space flights; and we set up all kinds of committees: astronautics, jet-flying engineering, the astronomy and biology of space flight, radio-control. Today people no longer scoff at our astronautics section, and its membership includes scientists, noted pilots, students, engineers and writers. Everyone is joining: young men and girls, middle-aged people and the elderly, pedants and dreamers.

As I was one of the organizers of the astronautics section, I happened to be on duty at the Club during the year when the first artificial earth satellite was put into orbit. I had been having a serious talk with two girls and a young man who were all hoping to fly not just anywhere, but to Mars. They had just left me and I was going through some letters that had arrived. One of them from a young man was most interesting.

"I'm eighteen," he wrote, "and have just finished school. So far I've done nothing of interest, but I would very much like to do something for science. I've heard it is intended to send up a dog in the artificial earth satellite. It would be much more important for science if a man was sent up. Please tell me how I can offer my services for an experimental flight into outer space. I'm sure I could radio back all my sensations.... And I shall be able to see the Earth as it looks from the stars!"

Another letter was from a woman. "I'm 46 and a housewife. I've done so little in my life. Let me serve science and offer myself for a study of the state of the human organism during space flight. I quite understand that not every rocket can return to earth...."

An engine-driver from Transbaikal wrote: "I'm very fond of mechanical things. I have a good understanding of machinery and am willing to learn. I might be useful as one of a crew in a space-ship...."

Actually there are already tens of thousands of people here in the Soviet Union and abroad who are longing to join in the space flights of the future.

Sitting there in the club I pondered over this astonishing side of the human character. What was this force that drew man to the stars and away from the Earth? Just the unbridled, insatiable, unconquerable thirst for knowledge! The same force that impelled the passionate, courageous polar explorers, some of whom fell only to rise again, some of whom perished, but who nevertheless struggled on through impenetrable ice, blizzards and frost towards the mysterious spot that is indicated by a white spot on the globe and is called the Pole. The same force impelled courageous ocean navigators to venture through the wide expanses and fierce storms of the oceans to discover unexplored lands that were splendid because they were unknown. The same force that drives a galaxy of daring, courageous climbers up icy slopes to inaccessible, unconquered mountain peaks, where there is nothing but raging winds, where the dazzling brightness blinds you and there is a cleansing, intoxicating, positive sense of tremendous height.

The aims and heights towards which man strives today are out of all comparison with what has already been achieved. . . .

This is the very nature of man, it is this that makes him splendid!

I first caught sight of him through the window as he was crossing the grounds of the Air Club. I was just about to go home, but had delayed, almost as though I felt he was coming to see me. There was something strange about him. I can't remember whether or not it was the way he walked, as he came up to the entrance.

The feeling increased when I looked at him at close range (as it turned out, he was actually coming to visit me!). It was not because he was short and his movements seemed awkward, nor because his body, arms and legs were somewhat out of proportion, nor even because his head was large, conical and completely bald. It was the look in his wise, large eyes, distorted by the remarkable, incredibly convex lenses of his spectacles. They brought closer to me his huge, rather sad eyes, which seemed to bore into me, to comprehend everything. At the back of my mind I attributed the impression he made on me to these strange spectacles.

I invited him to take a seat.

He smiled kindly as he looked at me and laid a thick manuscript on the table in front of me. He had obviously seen the fear in my eyes; perhaps he had even realized that I have a tendency to fight shy of manuscripts, I have to read so many of them in general. . . .

"No, literary consultation is not required, nor is the manuscript for the press," he remarked.

I looked inquiringly at him.

"I know it's a little premature to be talking about a definite inter-planetary flight, the possible composition of the crew. Though you are no doubt being besieged with requests. Still, I should already like to enlist the support of your section."

The individual confronting me was not a young man. I could not fob him off with a joke. I could not advise him to make a study of the fields of science which would one day make him a useful astronaut.

In some incomprehensible way he understood my feelings, for he said he was neither an astronaut, a geologist, a doctor nor an engineer, although—he seemed almost to stop breathing for a second—although he could become any one of them. All the same, he was counting on our support; he wanted to be sure that he would be one of the crew of the first space-ship to fly to Mars, because everyone had the right to . . . return!

I became quite uneasy. I remembered reading, in 1940, a letter from the manager of a department store in Sverdlovsk who had also asked to be assisted to return to Mars! It was said that in all other respects the man was a perfectly normal person.

My visitor smiled. I read in his eyes that he had again understood me.

Good God! I thought. Perhaps it was really true that the atmosphere in Mars is extremely rarefied and that long ago its inhabitants had abandoned the method of transmitting thoughts by means of sound waves, that is, by means of air vibrations. I caught myself imagining that not only could he guess my thoughts, but that I could guess his. The best thing to do was to regard him as a sick man.

"Yes," continued my visitor. "In the early days I found myself in a lunatic asylum, until I realized it was quite useless to try to convince people."

I wondered whether it was perhaps his letter that I had read some time before the war.

My visitor pointed to the manuscript.

"I could have written it in Russian or English, French or Dutch, in German, Chinese or Japanese, using one of the written languages current on this earth."

Trying to be civil, I unrolled the manuscript and frowned over the pages peppered with strange hieroglyphics. What was it? A mystery, or a symptom of disease?

"It is impossible," continued the visitor, "for a rational being, no matter who he is, to conceive in solitude an unknown language with all the appropriate turns of expression and flexibility, which would be capable even of transmitting thoughts and feelings that people cannot fully understand; neither is it possible for a rational being, in the same solitude, to invent a written language in which to write down all the wealth of such a language. You will understand that this manuscript could only have been written by a representative of an actually existing, distant, ancient, sagacious race living in the severe world of the faded past. . . ."

"But how can anyone read it!" I asked, unable to restrain myself, and at once observed the kindly sympathy behind the remarkable spectacles.

"In the course of the last century, culture on the Earth has developed by fits and starts. A path has been traversed from knowledge of the law of the conservation of energy to the utilization of the energy of matter, from idol worship to the making of machines which multiply the power of the brain and can replace it in certain definite functions. I am happy to be able to consider myself a contemporary of the blossoming of this culture on a bounteous and young planet which, having sufficient mass, loses neither atmosphere nor water and does not expect to fade away."

"And you think that an electronic computer could decipher the manuscript?" I asked, catching my visitor's meaning.

"Your machines will read the manuscript and you will understand who wrote it."

I almost knew already, I was prepared to understand who had written it. I sensed the stupidity or the strangeness of the situation, my hands were trembling even. Who would be interested in this encounter: the whole wide world or merely a handful of psychiatrists?

His thought-transmitting, thought-reading eyes watched me through the convex glasses. How could I be false, two-faced, hypocritical!

We parted after agreeing to meet again in six months' time in the same room.

And later . . . later I set out on a cruise in the *Georgy Sedov*. You've been spending several months with me in this ship's saloon.

"Just a minute!" cried Netayev, almost indignantly. His pale, goggling eyes looked up at me. "What about the manuscript?"

Noisy talk broke out in the saloon.

"Stories about madmen are always entertaining, somehow," someone remarked.

Netayev turned angrily on the speaker.

"In my opinion, the story's not finished," said the captain. He looked expectantly at me.

"I suppose it isn't," I concurred. "I shall be seeing him again."

"And have you the manuscript with you? May we look at it?" asked Netayev, eagerly.

"No, I haven't got it with me. The story actually has a continuation. Soon after our encounter a world-famous scientist called in at the Writers' Union. He is held in respect by the mathematicians of the world. A most interesting chap, the new type of scientist! Tall, upstanding, with the build of an athlete, plays chess and is very knowledgeable about literature. We were always arguing on literary subjects. He was only sixteen when he entered university. At twenty he already had a post graduate science degree and at twenty-eight became an academician."

"I know whom you mean!" exclaimed Netayev.

"Well, this scientist told us all about electronic computing machines. Of course, you've heard about cybernetic machines that can not only perform the most difficult mathematical calculations that it would take a man several generations to do, but also solve problems of logic. They have what's called an electronic memory, a sort of automatic dictionary, and they can translate from one language into another and even edit their own translations.

"Now, while I was driving the academician home in my car, he told me of a daring experiment he had made. He had given the great electronic computer of the Academy of Sciences—which, incidentally, could play a fair game of chess and even solve chess problems, but ... not studies built on paradoxes—he had given this machine a programme in accordance with which it had to guess the subject of a play from no more than the dramatis personae. This was all very amusing, only when the play was dull and trite with nothing at all new in it, the machine perfectly accurately indicated who was bad, who was good, at what point the assistant-lecturer betrays the girl student, when the noble professor intervenes and how it all comes out all right in the end....

"But—so the academician told me—the electronic computer possessed yet another valuable property. It could perform hundreds of thousands of operations a second and would soon be able to perform up to a million a second. By the process of exhaustion, the variation method, and using a tremendous number of operations, thousands of millions of operations, it could decipher any secret code in a very short space of time. According to the academician, the electronic computer could decipher Egyptian hieroglyphics or ancient cuneiform script far more rapidly than scientists could in the last century.

"That, as you can guess, is just what I was waiting for!

"Tentatively, I told the academician about my strange visitor and his manuscript. Immediately he burst into loud, infectious laughter. I was overcome with embarrassment and for a while simply concentrated on driving the car. By now we were in Bolshaya Kaluzhskaya Street and he soon had to get out. When he did, he extended his arm through the car door to shake my hand. As he pressed it, he gave me a rather mischievous look.

" 'Let's take the risk,' he said. 'We've got an experimental machine that is not used during the night. If you're able to convince my young colleagues, they'll be full of enthusiasm. Then we might try deciphering the first few pages.'

" 'And what about the remaining pages?' I pressed.

"Again his infectious laughter rang out.

" 'If it's at all possible to decipher them.'

"He laughed again, this young academician who loved chess problems and mathematical tricks with dramas. It was he who suggested I should try to persuade his young colleagues, yet when I presented myself to him at the Academy of Sciences, I found them already thoroughly roused by their indefatiga-

157

ble chief and waiting impatiently for me. They hurled themselves on the manuscript and began turning the pages and arguing about the programme they should feed to the machine to get them deciphered.

"What a business it was with the deciphering programme! You'd never guess the number of times it had to be changed!"

"Then it didn't work?" Netayev inquired anxiously.

"Absolutely nothing came of it. Several of the research people lost heart. But the academician continued to laugh and banter; then ... he took a hand and produced another programme."

"And what happened?"

"Months went by and—would you believe it—the academician continued to say that if we only tried hard enough we could get the cybernetic computer to decipher the city's night lights in the form of a poem. I don't know whether it was something to do with the peculiar features of the theory of probability or what it was, but one fine day we began to get something. The academician no longer bantered, but became angry and exacting. Now the machine was made to operate throughout the day as well as at night. Some delay was caused by calculations connected with filtering water through a dam. Someone raised a row about it.... In great agitation we added up the already rational conceptions and set the machine a programme again with more confidence."

"And you were able to read it?" asked Netayev, panting with excitement.

"Er, ye-es. The first few pages."

"Well, and what then? Stop tormenting us!"

"Well, the electronic computer, which increases the capacity of the human brain just like a steam excavator increases the power of human muscles, this machine deciphered the first pages of a *diary* written day after day, here on the Earth, by a

Martian who had been left behind in the taiga in tragic circumstances in the year 1908. . . .

"You can imagine my agitation as, through the eyes of a being from another world of arid deserts, I saw the bounteous, lavish beauty of our own planet with its infinite number of plants, the incomprehensible variety of which astounded the imagination of our strange visitor; with its animal world which has evolved through myriads of tiny, independent streams of life, each completely beautiful in its own way and, at the summit—man who has learned to understand nature. Then, to crown everything, this visitor, arrived from another planet, met this man.

"How astounded he must have been at the encounter! The creatures on the Earth were like him, like this inhabitant of far-distant Mars! That meant that the supreme rationality of evolution is narrow, for a rational being it can only select similar forms! These earthly beings, people, were able to think and they exchanged thoughts, although by a strange method, resorting to air vibrations, to sound, by means of which they could not only transmit their thoughts, but also conceal them. . . .

"He tried to imitate people, this visitor from another planet; he tried to produce sounds in order to tell people who he was. He did, indeed, tell them, but the Siberian merchants and village police merely took him for a foreigner, and an imbecile at that, and clapped him into a lunatic asylum.

"For half a century the Visitor from Outer Space lived among people, keeping his diary. We haven't read all the pages yet, but I promise to get them all deciphered and published in my novel *The Martian*, of which this story will be the beginning. In the Martian's diary, we shall be seeing through alien eyes, through the eyes of a representative of a wise and ancient race of beings, who on their decrepit planet reached the highest form of society, who passed our present phase of development millions of years ago. Through the eyes of the Martian we shall see our own life, ourselves, our actions and, laid bare by magic spectacles, the relations between people. We shall see lies and hypocrisy, which cannot exist when thoughts are not concealed by air vibrations ... and which will cease to exist when the spirit of the people has become adult.

"How did we appear to him during the early days of his association with us? And later, when he became our contemporary in two world wars: what did he think of those who decided arguments by shedding blood, who compelled people to work for them by force, who made some people happy, others miserable?

"When we read the Martian's diary we shall see life on the Earth as it is seen from outside!

"Then, in the last pages of the diary, we shall learn how much he had always longed to visit the country where people have begun to build the foundations of a society to which he is accustomed; we shall learn how, by living with the people, he came to change his opinion of them. Filled with admiration for the impetuous development of their culture, during one century of which a whole stage of history was traversed, a stage which required millions of years on Mars, the Martian dreams that the earthly beings, more successful and energetic than the beings of his own race, will return him to his rugged, but beloved Mars. He dreams of returning to Mars, taking with him the inexhaustible, vital energy that is finding outlet in our people, the energy that will help to prolong life on withering Mars for millions of years to come!

"We shall read his diary, we shall learn about his life on our Earth, what sort of a man he was! Or rather, what sort of a Martian he was!

"Yes, I'm thrilled at the prospect of another meeting with him. Will not all of us feel this thrill at the mere thought that we have by our side someone who has, as it were, come to us from our future and is judging us by the laws of our own aspirations! We do not want him to condemn us for anything, not for a single moment.

"And that's the end of my story."

"I'd love to read the whole diary," mused Netayev.

"I promise you, you shall," I assured him, and then I suddenly remembered something. "Half a minute, I thought we agreed that you weren't going to believe my story!"

Netayev smiled condescendingly, and the captain waggled a finger at me.

"If we don't go on the southern cruise, I should very much like to come and see the Air Club, when you're on duty on that particular day."

The saloon became noisy. People crowded round me asking me to write up my next encounter with the Martian, if it ever took place.

"Of course I'll write about it," I promised. "I'll write a novel."

"Why a novel?" asked someone indignantly. "You'll be writing about the Martian."

I went up on deck. The stars are simply wonderful in the Arctic. They seem to be closer than anywhere else.

Netayev was waiting for me.

"There it is, Mars!" he remarked, pointing to a reddish star.

As I gazed at the light from the unexplored world, I began to think.

"You know, if he were here, by our side, we should sometimes feel rather ashamed," said the navigation officer.

"But do you know why I told the story about him? Because

161

if he'd been with us in the saloon during our cruise, and had met the people in this story and listened to them talking, we should never have felt ashamed in his presence."

"D'you really think that?" asked Netayev earnestly.

For a long time we exchanged no more words; then Netayev spoke again.

"I say, d'you think they might bear me in mind at that astronautics section of yours? Stars are dear to the navigator. I could navigate in outer space too."

We decided to turn in.

But there was someone else laying in wait for me. The pilot. He wanted a word with me in confidence. Still, I'll give away his secret. After listening to what he had to say, I gave him a firm handshake.

After all, it is men like him who will be at the controls of the first space-ships.

The *Georgy Sedov* proceeded on its course under the stars.

G. GUREVICH

INFRA DRACONIS

A black circle floats over the shining sea of stars—a matte saucer with rather misty edges. At one edge the stars are eclipsed, only to be born again at the other edge half an hour later. Familiar constellations, only here they are brighter and their pattern more complicated and delicate. Only one of them—the Flying Fish—has an extra star, the brightest in the sky, the most beautiful—our own sun.

But we are not looking at the sun, or enjoying the delicate pattern of stellar embroidery. Our eyes are fixed on the black circle, although no details are distinguishable in the dense obscurity, either with the naked eye or through the telescope. There are six of us—the entire crew of a space-ship: Charushin, the old man leading the expedition whom we call Grandpa, the Varentsovs—husband and wife, the Yuldashevs—also husband and wife, and myself, Rady Blokhin.

"Well, shall we go back?" asked Grandpa Charushin.

"There's nothing for it," replied Tolya Varentsov, the chief engineer. "The rocket is adapted for landing on dry land, and over there it's water, nothing but ocean. We have hand lathes, home-made at that, and six people to work, all semi-skilled. We would be hanging about for a year contriving something and then we'd drown when making the landing on the water. We can't take the risk."

"What's more, our fuel's running out," added Rahim Yul-dashev. "We calculated it with you. A landing means a delay of seven years. We haven't enough air for an extra seven years. And we're not young."

Ayesha tugged at his sleeve. Rahim had forgotten it was not polite to mention age in front of Grandpa. The old man was already over ninety.

"After all, we won't be going back empty-handed," remarked Galya Varentsova.

Then Charushin put in a word.

"Then there's only one way out."

We looked at our chief, puzzled. Ayesha was the first to catch on to his meaning.

"On no account!" she almost shrieked.

———

"Life is measured in deeds, not words." I first heard Grandpa use the words seventeen years ago. I remember the first time I visited him. It was late autumn. There was a damp, penetrating wind. The pocket plane carried me over black fields of trampled grass, over bare trees, over the leaden waves of Kuibyshev Sea. Then I spied a bright blue fence on a clay escarpment, a little house of green, glassy brick, and an old man at the gate in a warm jacket of artificial ermine. His thick grey hair appeared to be whitish-grey as though it, too, was synthetic. I recognized him from a photograph. I switched off the pocket plane and landed awkwardly at his feet, straight into a ditch.

"Come and get changed, then you can introduce yourself," he said, offering me a hand.

That was my introduction to Pavel Alexandrovich Charushin, the famous space captain, one of the crew of the first flight to Venus, commander of the first expedition on the

Jupiter sputnik, first on Saturn, first on Neptune, and so on and so forth. Here on the shores of Kuibyshev Sea he was spending the last years of his glorious life.

I was myself connected with the stars, indirectly that is. By education I was a building engineer and worked on the construction of the Chief Inter-Planetary Station on Mount Kilimanjaro in East Africa. When a specialist finds himself in a strange sphere, he is tempted to alter things to suit himself. In addition I was young and self-confident. I was drawing up a plan for the reconstruction of the solar system. At that time, the beginning of the 21st century, it was already obvious that all the planets were unsuitable for habitation and almost all of them of no use to us. So I was suggesting they should be shuffled around. Venus and Mars were to be driven into the Earth's orbit, Mars to be supplied with an artificial atmosphere and Venus's atmosphere to be purified of carbonic acid gas. I had further proposed that Saturn, Uranus and Neptune should be split up into parts to reduce the force of gravity there, and the various parts driven singly closer to the Sun, by means of atomic explosions. I proposed settling a colony of explorers on Triton and sending them out on an inter-stellar cruise. According to my calculations, Triton could circumnavigate all the neighbouring stellar systems in about a thousand years. In addition I intended educating children on Jupiter in conditions of heightened gravity, so that their young bones and muscles would grow strong, and then they would all be strong men on the Earth.

To my great surprise all these magnificent projects were invariably turned down. However, I did not give up but stubbornly traipsed from one institution to the next and called on prominent experts. It was natural that I should also turn to Charushin, and so I went to the trouble of flying out to the Kuibyshev Sea Many people turned to him: young people who dreamed of working in outer space, authors of books, budding scientists, and the people of the local region whom he represented as a deputy. His name, too, constantly appeared in the newspapers. Charushin's signature was appended to the treaty on the Final Disarmament of Nations. At the world Peace Celebrations, Charushin travelled with Chinese, Americans and Germans on the first wagon-load of machine-guns and mortars en route to the open-hearth furnaces for smelting. Without doubt he was one of the most prominent people of his time.

Like many other people, the old man listened to what I had to say with a smile that was benevolently condescending.

"The trouble with you, Rady Grigoryevich," he said, "is that you're rushing too far ahead. There's no need for us to settle ourselves all over the solar system, there's enough room here on the Earth where it's comfortable. Your ideas will be needed in three hundred years' time. No doubt you say to yourself: see how perspicacious I am! And all to no purpose. No good comes of occupying yourself with problems not of our time. When it becomes necessary and possible, people will set about reconstructing the planets. And then they'll easily think of all the things you are so occupied with today."

I did not agree with the old man, but I did not take offence. I felt it was praiseworthy to live in the future in one's own thoughts. So I continued to bore Pavel Alexandrovich with the details of my project. With a smile, Grandpa tore holes in my ideas, but he invariably invited me over on my next free day. He probably liked my youthful cocksureness. And he found the country cottage a solitary place enough. It was different in the summer months when his grandchildren and great-grandchildren took possession of it and the chatter of children's voices filled the garden. But in the winter months there were only letters and telephone calls

So Pavel Alexandrovich used to listen to me and then I would listen to him dictating his famous memoirs to an electronic shorthand machine. They had just begun to be printed in the *Komsomolskaya Pravda*. You recall, of course, the beginning, the first few lines:

"Our expedition flew to the Moon to begin preparations for. . . ."

I remember saying to the old man at the time:

"You can't start off like that, Pavel Alexandrovich. People start their memoirs with childhood, the day of their birth, or even with a genealogical table. And here you are leaving out a quarter of your life and beginning: 'Our expedition flew. . . .'"

It was then I first heard him say:

"Rady, we space experts have our own way of counting. We measure life not in years, but in discoveries, explorations. So I've begun my book with the story of the first occurrence."

"But the reader is interested in knowing what sort of person you are, what your childhood was like and how you came to explore the planets."

The old man would not agree.

"You're wrong, young man. People are not interested in me, but in what I do. Every epoch has its favourite profession. One honours sailors, another—writers, airmen, inventors. We space navigators are the favourites of the twenty-first century; we are always remembered, are the first to be sent invitations, are given seats in the front row."

These words are to be found in the postscript to the first volume of the *Memoirs*, and also the following:

"I was lucky enough to be born at the dawn of the epoch of great discoveries in outer space. The years of my childhood coincided with the infancy of astronavigation. Before I reached manhood the Moon had been mastered by man. As a young man I dreamed of meeting Venus, as a mature man of years—Jupiter, as an old man—Old Man Neptune. Technical progress made my dreams come true. In less than a century, during my lifetime, speed increased from 8 to 800 kilometres a second. Man's command of space became immeasurably wider. In the middle of the last century he had one planet—a sphere with a radius of 6,300 kilometres; today he has a sphere with a radius of 4,000 million kilometres. We have become stronger and wiser; we have enriched physics, astronomy, geology, biology, by comparing our world with others. Only one dream has not been fulfilled: we have not met other rational beings. We have not grown tired, but at present it is not possible to go farther. We have already reached the limit of the solar system, visited all the planets, ahead of us now is inter-stellar space. A distance of four light hours has been covered, but it is four light years to the nearest star. We have a speed of 800 kilometres a second, we need a hundred times more. Obviously we shall not soon move to other suns, some people say we never shall. The photon rocket and other still bolder projects are so far only projects. The era of discoveries in outer space will suffer an interruption of probably three or four centuries.

People journeyed into outer space for various reasons. I, for example, as an engineer was attracted by the idea of building on an unprecedented planetary scale. And Pavel Charushin had hoped to discover rational beings. Hoping to meet them, he had flown off to discover new worlds. Now we had come to a dead end. There was nothing more to discover, and he did not want to become merely a cosmic pilot. Peace, honour, grandchildren, memoirs, the country home. ... And he would have ended his life there in a backwater, but for the sudden idea of the possibility of infra-suns that came into my head.

Actually it was he who in some measure suggested the idea to me; he could not reconcile himself to the idea that there was nowhere else to fly to.

How did I reason it out?

To the limits of the solar system it is four light hours, to the nearest star—four light years. A vast ocean of void. But is it certain that it is all void? We only know that there are no bright stars there, otherwise they would be visible. But perhaps there are dark, not bright, bodies there. Perhaps our celestial maps, like most of our terrestrial maps, indicate only the star-capitals, and leave out the star-villages.

Take, for example, a sphere with a diameter of 15 light years. There will be four suns in it—our Sun, Alpha-Centaurus, Sirius and Procyon. We can reckon that there are seven suns, because apart from our own, all the others are double stars.

But in the same area of space there are some scores of feeble, dim stars—red-dwarfs, sub-dwarfs, white-dwarfs. These are the stars near to us, but almost all of them are invisible to the naked eye and it was only in the twentieth century that we learned that they are so near.

Thus, there are isolated stars visible to the naked eye, and dozens more visible through the telescope. Could there not be in the same space hundreds of heavenly bodies which the telescope has not noticed? It is, of course, terribly difficult, among the thousand million feeble stars known to us, to pick out a hundred small ones that are near us!

And the temperatures suggest the same conclusion.

In the world of stars the rule is: the larger the star, the hotter it is; the smaller—the cooler. The red-dwarfs are ten times smaller than the Sun, their temperature is 2000°-3000°C. Let us suppose that there exist some bodies ten times smaller than the red-dwarfs. What would their temperature be? Probably 1000°, 600°, 300° or 100°C. The luminosity of the largest would be insignificant, that of the others—nil. With a temperature of less than 600°, bodies send out only invisible infra-red rays. Invisible, dark black suns! And among them of special interest to us dark, warm planets heated from within, with a surface temperature of 30°C above zero.

Why have they not been found before? Partly because no one looked for them, partly because it was difficult to find them. In general, from the Earth it is impossible to see dark planets. For our earth radiates infra-red light, we live in a sea of infra-red flame. It is hardly possible to live in a flame and yet notice the light of a distant small star!

Timidly, I outlined all this to Pavel Alexandrovich. Out of the corner of my eye I watched the condescending smile fade from the old man's face, the shaggy eyebrows form into a frown. I thought I was reasoning so logically. Could there be some unforeseen objection? I somehow floundered on to the end; then I waited to be routed.

"Now that is interesting, Rady," he began. "A planet heated internally, a world inside out. And everything different from what is on the Earth. There will be life there, don't you think? Of course, if there is no light, there cannot be vegetation. But animal life? On the Earth there are animals that live in darkness, in caves and in the ocean depths. The animal world in general is older than that of plants. But higher forms, what about them? Can higher forms arise in eternal darkness?"

Then he burst out laughing and clapped me on the shoulder.

"Perhaps you and I will be off into outer space again, Rady! Are you ready to fly off in search of your infras?"

"What about you, Pavel Alexandrovich?"

He chose to interpret the question in his own way and was offended.

"Why not? I'm not old yet. I'm still not eighty. And our statistics put middle age at ninety-two and a half years."

* * *

Even I was astonished when, six months later, the Central Lunar Observatory announced the discovery of the first infra.

Without Pavel Alexandrovich, all this would have happened much later. But he abandoned all his affairs and diversions. He stripped the greenhouse of its luxuriant flowers and turned it into a workshop. He dropped the memoirs in the middle of a sentence. The electronic shorthand machine did nothing but write letters to scientific and public bodies, to old friends interested in outer space, to comrades, pupils, to the Moon, Mars, Yunon and Io, to long-distance space-ships, all with the convincing, insistent, enthusiastic request to organize a search for black suns.

I had to admire the old man's energy. It was as though he had only been waiting for the signal while sitting at home in his country cottage. Perhaps he really was waiting. And then the great aim arrived—undiscovered worlds: he could fly off into outer space, he could search and make discoveries.

Infras were found in the constellations of Lyra, Sagittarius, the Little Bear, Tucana, Telescopium. . . . And the nearest and most interesting for us was in the constellation of Draco, the dragon. Its surface temperature was 10°C above zero, the distance to it was "only" seven light days. "Only" forty times as far as to Neptune. A space-rocket could cover the distance in fourteen years.

A year later the rocket took off. In it were the Varentsovs, the Yuldashevs, Pavel Alexandrovich and myself. Only I know what it cost the old man to persuade the authorities to include himself and me in the crew. In his case, age was against him, in mine—my youth and inexperience.

* * *

The first days of the flight were just like my first excursion to Moscow: enthrallingly interesting, everything perfectly familiar. I had read about it all a hundred times and seen it all a hundred times at the cinema. From a height, the Earth appears as a gigantic globe casting a shadow across the sky. Fourfold gravity, then the miracle of weightlessness. The Moon was a strange, black-and-white world, its face pock-marked. Smooth lunar leaps, deep black shadows, abysses, age-old dust. I had read about it, imagined it; now I saw it and was astounded. Then came the monotonous days of our every-day life, which the writers omit from their descriptions. A tiny sleeping-cabin, three metres by three, hammocks, a table, a cupboard. Beyond its wall, a work-room just a trifle larger containing a telescope, the control panel, instruments, computers. Farther on—the stores, the engine-room and half a kilometre of cans with fuel. If you like, you can take a walk alongside the cans; if you like, you can get into a flying-suit and tumble about in space. Then once more the hammock, the table and cupboard. In fact—a prison cell. Thirty years in solitary confinement.

Darkness and the stars, the stars and darkness. There are 24 divisions on our watches, otherwise we could get confused. Day or night, there is no difference. Electricity by day in the cabin, at night—more electricity. Stars through the windows by day, stars by night. Silence. Peace. Yet actually we are flying—a state of steady movement in a straight line. Almost one and a half million kilometres an hour, 35 million each day. We write up the log: "May 23, we have traversed a thousand million kilometres. June 1, we have crossed Saturn's orbit." When that happened we had a ceremonial dinner, sang songs and celebrated. But actually it was a purely conventional milestone because there was nothing but void before reaching the orbit and nothing but void after it. In point of fact the orbit itself was far away on one side of us. And Saturn was no more clearly seen than from the Earth, looking like an ordinary little star.

It was Pavel Alexandrovich who devised all kinds of ceremonies. He was a past master at filling up the hours. Even in the space-rocket there was never enough time for him. After sleeping—space drill for at least an hour. Without this the muscles would become atrophied from the perpetual weightlessness. Then a compulsory airing in space, an examination of the rocket first externally, then internally. Work at the telescope. Dinner. Then two hours during which he dictated his reminiscences. He dictated to me. We had been unable to take the electronic shorthand machine with us on account of the extra weight. Then reading from microbooks. Grandpa read for one hour exactly and always laid the book aside at the end of it. It was partly recreation, and at the same time a struggle to keep our spirits up. "We must patiently wait for the morrow," he said frequently. As for me, I did my best to follow his example. I realized it could not be otherwise. If one indulged in bad temper, then one let oneself go. First it would be spleen, then laziness, then illness. Then one would give up working and forget one's duties. There had been tragedies in outer space: people had allowed themselves to become demoralised and had even been known to turn back before reaching the goal.

Work was the only cure for spleen. But there was not much work to do. Inspection and running repairs do not take up much time. I used to work on my plan for reconstructing the planets, but more for my own satisfaction than anything else. One cannot, in isolation, outdo such a mighty collective as mankind. And with each year of our flight my knowledge became more and more out of date by the standards on Earth. There they were forging ahead, but I knew nothing of it.

The only rational occupation was astronomical observations. We compiled a catalogue, measured the distances to the stars. Usually they are measured by a triangle. The base of the triangle is the diameter of the Earth's orbit, the two angles— the direction to the star. The height—the distance to the star—is determined by the side and the two angles. But the narrower and longer the triangle, the greater the possible error, hence this method is only suitable for the nearest stars. It was easier for us—we were now a thousand times farther from the Sun, the base of our triangle was a thousand times larger, the distances could be measured a thousand times more accurately. That applies, roughly speaking, to all the stars that are visible in the telescope. Here then was an occupation to last us for the whole journey: measuring and calculating, measuring and calculating. Then the entries in the log-book: Catalogue No. so and so, spectral class AO, distance—7118 light years. Sometimes as we wrote we would get infuriated. We were spending a whole lifetime on seven light days, and here we were dealing with seven thousand light years. No one would ever fly such a distance, to this sun of class AO.

Boredom, tedious monotony, and yet—continual vigilance. Nothing happens for whole years, yet every second might bring a catastrophe. For space is not entirely empty, there were meteorites and meteorite dust flying about. At the speed at which we were travelling even gas clouds would be dangerous; it could be like plunging into water. We did encounter in outer space some dense zones unknown to science. When we entered them, everything started shifting and one's chest felt constricted. It is not clear why. Meteorite dust corrodes the sheathing, metal gets fatigued, and stray currents appear.

So gradually everything wears out. Then we find an air leak, or the steering goes out of order, or the instruments let us down. For years nothing happens, then suddenly.... Consequently, someone has to be on duty all the time.

The hours of solitary duty are worst of all. You think of the Earth. You want to walk in the fields and woods. You want to see moondaisies in bloom and larks singing in the blue sky. You long for crowds, the Metro, the sports stadium, meetings. You want to hear loud shouting, not silence, to have your elbows jostled by the crowds round you, lots and lots of people, all strangers to you, and women and girls. You close your eyes—the Red Square, the Kremlin, demonstrations, bright banners ... you open your eyes—the hammock, the table, the cupboard and through the window the stars and darkness.

And so day after day, month after month. There were six of us in the space rocket. We worked in shifts, keeping watch for two years, sleeping for four. Artificial sleep, of course, with cooling.

I could stand being awakened all right, but Grandpa not so well. After all, he was an old man, his heart was wearing out. The first time it passed off all right, but after the second, he had fainting fits, pains round the heart, pain in the left shoulder. For four hours our doctor, Ayesha, nursed him. Then she announced that if he undertook a third shift, she would not answer for the consequences.

———

For fourteen years we had been hurtling towards an invisible point and at last the moment came when we could distinguish the goal—a small dark circle that eclipsed the stars. We had arrived accurately at our goal. The observations of the astronomers on the Earth had been correct. But one thing they had not foreseen: it turned out that Infra Draconis was not a single, but a twin body. There were two black suns there—A and B. A was smaller, B slightly larger. A was nearer to us, B a little farther away. "A little" in cosmic terms, of course. Actually the distance between them was greater than the distance from the Earth to Saturn.

We were all bursting with impatience and especially Pavel Alexandrovich, although he showed no sign of it. He had already prepared a whole arsenal for inter-planetary conversations: light signals, infra-red searchlights. There was also an alphabet with pictures in relief, a collection of geometrical figures.

The great day of our encounter arrived.

In the morning we began to put on the brake. Top and bottom appeared, things forgotten in the air fell on the floor. By midday the dark Infra spot began to grow perceptibly, the stars were extinguished one after the other. Finally, the black saucer hung before us. We came to a halt. We had become Infra's temporary satellite.

Then, imagine our disappointment: our astronomers had made a slight error. They had determined the surface temperature as 10°C above zero, but it turned out to be 6°C below. There were gases in the atmosphere: methane and ammonia as on Jupiter, carbon dioxide as on Venus, a great deal of hydrogen and water vapour—dense clouds. Beneath them was a frozen ocean—ice, snow-fields, ice-hummocks. The ice was tens and hundreds of kilometres thick. We used explosives to measure it.

Was it worth while flying for fourteen years to see an ordinary arctic night!

Grandpa was thoroughly despondent. The last attempt had failed! The dream of his life had not come true.

It was then we came to the decision to visit Infra B as well.

At first glance this seemed natural enough. We were near it, so why not go there. But outer space has its own basis of calculation. There everything depends on fuel. On the Earth, fuel determines the distance traversed, the kilometres, but in outer space it determines only the speed. Fuel is not spent all the time, only when taking off and slowing down. Most frequently enough is taken for two take-offs and for slowing down twice. To visit the second Infra meant delaying our return for three or four years. We did not want to add extra years to the journey, but where thirty years have already been spent, three years do not count much. None of us wished to turn his back on the unexplored world.

For a whole year we slowly crept from one Infra to the other, and now the black spot had enlarged and become a coal-black disc. We slowed down again, became a temporary satellite, and sent the automatic scout into the darkness. We saw for ourselves, for this time the darkness was not complete. There was summer lightning and at times storms in the atmosphere. Cloud contours were visible on the screen. A radio report came from the automatic scout—the air temperature was 24°C above zero. Perhaps astronomers on the Earth had made their mistake because they had combined the rays from the ice-bound Infra with this stormy Infra. It turned out that an average of 10°C above zero was not so far off the truth.

But we must have omitted something in our calculations, for we lost our scout rocket; apparently it sank. At the last moment we saw an expanse of water and high, slanting waves on the television screen. We sent out a second rocket which flew several times round Infra. We saw clouds and rain—falling straight, not slanting as it usually does on the Earth. Even the drops on Infra were heavier. Again we saw waves. It was only sea, sea everywhere, not a single islet. An ocean at the equator and an ocean at the poles. No ice at all. That was understandable Warmth comes from the interior on In-fra, and the climate there is the same everywhere, not colder at the poles.

There were no continents. no islands, not even the summit of a volcano. Ocean, ocean everywhere.

What a vast number of surprises there are in this outer space; it is incorrect to speak of monotonous uniformity and boredom. What was it we had counted on? That there would be dry land and oceans on the Infras, just as there are on the Earth. Rational beings (and in our hearts we had all hoped to meet them) can only develop on dry land, naturally. We intended making a study of the ocean, but only from the coast; to swim out and let down a small bathysphere. And our star-plane could only land on terra firma.

And so now a black circle floats over the shining sea of stars —a matte saucer with rather misty edges. At one edge the stars are eclipsed, only to be born again at the other edge half an hour later. Familiar constellations, only they are brighter and their pattern more complicated. Only one of them has an extra star—our own Sun.

But we were not looking at the Sun, or enjoying the delicate pattern of stellar embroidery. Our eyes were fixed on the black circle, although no details are distinguishable in the dense obscurity, either with the naked eye or with a telescope

"Well, shall we go back?" asked Grandpa Charushin.

For the hundredth and thousandth time the same question is asked. Yes, we shall have to go back, we cannot contrive anything to meet the situation.

"Then there's only one way out," Grandpa announced.

We looked at our chief, puzzled. Ayesha was the first to catch on to his meaning.

178

"On no account," she almost shrieked "I know, you want to go down in the bathysphere."

We were all filled with consternation. It was quite possible to make the descent in the bathysphere, but the question was how to return. The automatic scout cannot fly. The bathysphere would remain there for ever . . . and with a man inside it.

"We simply won't let you!" insisted Ayesha.

But Grandpa merely shrugged his shoulders.

"You know, Ayesha," he said, "you're stuffed with medical prejudice. You imagine a man only has the right to die of some serious illness. We space experts have our own calculation of life. We measure it in deeds, not years."

"It's an unnecessary sacrifice!" declared Rahim. "We must work consistently, return to the Earth and report. The next expedition will be specially prepared and will make a study of the bed of the ocean."

The next! But when? In thirty years' time?

Tolya Varentsov was about to intervene and volunteer to go himself. Galya seized him by the sleeve. Then I insisted that I should be the candidate.

"The decision has been made," announced Grandpa. "So don't waste time arguing about nothing. I command you to start preparations for the descent."

———

The last preparations were in progress, yet we still could hardly take it all in. The eve of the take-off arrived. The old captain gave orders for a farewell supper; he drew up the menu himself. We played our favourite record—from the newsfilm *On the Streets of Moscow*. Then we listened to Beethoven's Ninth Symphony. The old man was fond of it because it was a rousing symphony, a call to struggle. We drank champagne. It's quite a problem, drinking champagne in a weightless rocket; it has a habit of floating away into the air. Then we sang songs. Our outer space hymn, no one knows who composed it:

> Perhaps we need eternity
> To discover the whole of infinity
> But before the goal is reached
> The captain departs from us,
> But others will be found, if need be....

Ayesha and Galya wept. I got a bit tipsy and asked: "But aren't you scared, Pavel Alexandrovich?" And he replied: "Rady, young man, I'm terrified, but most of all I'm afraid I'm doing all this in vain, and I'll see nothing but black water...." I gripped his hand and said: "Pavel Alexandrovich, it's true there may be nothing at all. Take back your orders, please!"

———

And now there were only five of us, standing with lips compressed in front of the loud speaker, which was emitting a sound of rolling thunder, whistling, hooting, howling. The atmosphere of Infra is saturated with electricity, that's the obstacle.

At last Charushin's calm voice broke through the din of atmospherics. Our Grandpa was with us! The familiar husky bass filled the cabin.

"I've switched off the searchlight," he was saying. "It's not absolutely dark. There is sheet and forked lightning all the time. By the light of the flashes, flat clouds like a blanket can be seen. They are like those on Jupiter. Cumulus clouds at the edges. The air is dense and there are whirlwinds at the edges of the air streams."

There were more atmospherics; isolated words and whole phrases were inaudible. Then audibility improved.

"The air is becoming clearer," said Grandpa. "I see the sea. An enamel-black surface. Small waves like ripples. I'm falling slowly, the air is very dense. The gravity is incredible, it's difficult to move. It's the same as on the Infra glaciers. It's even difficult to move my tongue."

Suddenly there was a joyful exclamation:

"Birds! Luminescent birds! Another, and another. Three at once. They flashed by and were gone. Does the television screen shot it? I managed to see a round head, thick body and small, fluttering wings. They look rather like our flying fish. Perhaps they are fish, and not birds. But they were flying high."

A heavy splash, then a pause.

"Did you hear that noise? It was me, falling into the water. I struck it hard. Still, it doesn't matter. I've switched off the light. I'm getting accustomed to the darkness."

And then a little later:

"I'm going down slowly, at the rate of two metres a second. I've switched on the searchlight again. Through the window there's fiery blizzard—shining whirlwinds, waves, clouds. What a lot of small creatures there are here! Probably similar to our shrimps. The deeper I go, the thicker they are. It's just the opposite on the Earth, where life is scarcer deep down. But there, the warmth comes from the top, here it's from below.

"And what's this? Long and dark, no head, no tail. A whale, a sperm-whale? It moves quickly, a shining stream in its wake. A row of lights along the sides, portholes as it were. Could it be a submarine? Or something else, not comparable to anything. I'll give it a signal from the searchlight in any case: two-two-four, two-three-six, two-two-four.

"It paid no attention. It has gone off to the right. It's out of sight.

"Here are some more monsters—something between a turtle and an octopus. I'm calling them octopuses by way of comparison, actually they have five legs. Five tentacles, one at the back like a rudder, four at the sides. The ends are thickened, with suckers. One of the front tentacles has a strong luminous organ. Like a headlight. Its straight beam is shining on seaweeds. It has a carapace on its back. It has crab-like eyes on movable stalks. The mouth is trumpet-shaped. I'm describing it in such detail because these creatures are swimming towards me. Now they are looking straight into my headlight. It's an eerie feeling—the look in their eyes is perfectly intelligent, the pupil has a crystalline lens, and the iris gives a phosphorescent, dead-green light, like that of a cat. I once read that the terrestrial octopus has a human look in its eyes, but I've never seen one, so can make no comparison.

"The searchlight is sweeping the ocean bed. There are some knotted roots on it, like corals or sea lilies. I can see thick stems, little cups hang downwards from their branches, some resting on the bottom. Our sea lilies hold their cups upwards, they catch descending food. What are these looking for in the silt? Decaying remains? But they don't all reach to the bottom. Could they be absorbing warmth? But then they are plants. Plants without light? It's impossible. Incidentally, there is infra-red light coming from the ocean bed. Is it possible to use the energy of infra-red rays to construct albumen, decompose carbon dioxide? There's not much energy, it needs to be accumulated. But green leaves on the Earth also accumulate energy. Actually, visible rays do not of themselves decompose carbon dioxide.

"I've had a delay," continued the old man. "I'm caught in the weeds on the bottom. I can look around at my leisure.

I'm more and more convinced that there are plants below me. Here's a fat, headless fish chewing at the shoots. Another—toothy and long—has seized the fat one and has swum upwards. The flow of food here goes from the bottom to the surface. The luminescent birds in the last instance."

There was a sound of scraping and dull thuds on metal. What did it signify?

"The bathysphere has shifted," announced Grandpa "Something has seized it and is dragging at it. I can't see what. There's nothing in front of the headlight.

"The sea bed slopes. There's no end to the weeds. But the strange thing is that the plants are in straight rows as in an orchard. Something enormous is slowly moving, cutting down whole bushes at the roots. The voracious monster is swallowing the bushes. I can't see very well, somewhere to the side this living combine is creeping along. There's a heap of rock ahead. We've sailed through it. A black chasm. The bathysphere is going down. The pressure is increasing. Goodbye! Greetings to Moscow!"

A second's pause. Then suddenly a shout, almost a yell

"A crack!!!"

There was a sound of ever more frequent ringing blows Evidently water had burst into the chamber.

The old man gulped. Probably he had swallowed some water, too. Then a stream of words came tumbling out in swift succession.

"There are buildings at the bottom of the chasm. A town. Street-lights. A dome, spheres. Swimming turrets. Strange creatures . . . they're everywhere. . . . Can they possibly be. . . ."

A loud crash. A cry of pain. A gurgling sound.

Then the triumphant, prolonged howling and loud whistling of atmospheric interference.

In profound silence five people watched the black circle though there was nothing to be distinguished with the naked eye or through the telescope.

"We'll come back here in thirty years' time," said Tolya Varentsov, now chief of the expedition. And Galya softly sang:

> *Perhaps we need eternity*
> *To discover the whole of infinity*
> *But before the goal is reached*
> *The captain departs from us,*
> *But others will be found, if need be....*

Will they be found?

VLADIMIR SAVCHENKO

PROFESSOR BERN'S AWAKENING

In 1952, when the greatest stupidity of the twentieth century, the "cold war," had the whole world in its grip, a vast
audience of people heard Professor Bern quote Einstein's
gloomy epigram: "If world war three is fought with atom
bombs, then world war four will be fought with clubs...."

This created a more powerful impression than a common-
place witticism would have done, coming as it did from Professor Bern, who was known as "the most universal scientist
of the twentieth century." A flood of letters followed, but
Bern was unable to reply to them; he died in the autumn of
the same year, while on his second geophysical expedition to
Central Asia.

Engineer Niemayer, who was his sole companion on this
little expedition declared later:

"We had moved our base by helicopter to the interior of
the Gobi desert. When the instruments and explosives for
seismological investigations had been loaded, the professor set
off on the first trip. I was to stay behind to see to the rest of
the equipment. As the helicopter was taking off, something
went wrong with the engine. It began to misfire and finally
stopped altogether. The helicopter had not yet got up speed,
so it rapidly dropped vertically from an altitude of a hundred
metres. As it struck the ground there were two violent explosions. The descent had been so precipitate that the sudden
impact must have detonated the kieselguhr—dynamite. Pro-

fessor Bern, the helicopter and everything in it were literally blasted to bits. . . ."

Word for word, Niemayer repeated the story to correspondents crowding round him, adding nothing, omitting nothing. The experts found it convincing. Indeed, since a loaded helicopter loses height abnormally rapidly in the hot, rarefied air of a desert high up in the mountains, the impact on striking the ground could have just such tragic consequences. The commission which flew out to investigate the catastrophe confirmed these suggestions. Niemayer alone knew that this was not actually what happened. But even on his deathbed he continued to keep Professor Bern's secret.

The spot in the Gobi desert which Bern's expedition reached was in no way different from its surroundings. The same hard waves of sand-hills, indicating the direction in which the last wind had driven them; the same grey-golden sand crunching underfoot, gritty to the teeth; the same sun, white and blinding by day, purple-crimson towards nightfall, and describing an almost vertical arc in the sky each day. Not a tree or bird; not a wisp of cloud, not even the smallest pebble in the sand.

As soon as they reached their goal and found the shaft dug out during an earlier expedition, Professor Bern set fire to the page of his notebook which recorded the exact location of the site. Now only one thing distinguished this desert spot from its surroundings: the presence there of Bern and Niemayer. They were lounging in deck-chairs outside the tent. Not far away the silvery fuselage and propeller blades of the helicopter shone in the sun, looking like a huge dragon-fly that had settled on the desert sands. The last rays of the sun were almost horizontal and tent and helicopter cast peculiar, long shadows across the sand-hills.

"A medical man in the Middle Ages once suggested a

simple means of prolonging life indefinitely," Professor Bern was saying. "All you have to do is to freeze yourself and remain in that state in a cellar somewhere for ninety or a hundred years. Then you warm yourself up and come alive again. You could live for ten years in one century and then freeze yourself again until better times. . . . True, for some reason the doctor himself had no desire to live for an extra thousand years and died a natural death in his sixties." Bern screwed up his eyes with their merry twinkle, cleaned his cigarette-holder and fitted in another cigarette.

"Hm, the Middle Ages. . . . Our unbelievable twentieth century is busy carrying out the craziest of the ideas of the Middle Ages. Radium is now the philosopher's stone for converting mercury or lead into gold. We've not yet invented perpetual motion—it's all against the laws of nature—but we've discovered eternal and self-renewing sources of nuclear energy. . . . And then, another of their ideas: in 1666 almost all Europe was expecting the end of the world. In those days the reason for it was merely the cabbalistic meaning of the number 666 and blind faith in the Apocalypse, but today there is a solid basis for the end of the world idea owing to the atomic and hydrogen bombs. But to return to freezing. . . . The mediaeval doctor's naïve idea has scientific meaning nowadays. You've heard of anabiosis, haven't you? Leeuwenhoek discovered it in 1701. It means slowing down life processes by means of cold or dehydration. You see, cold and absence of humidity seriously reduce the rate of all chemical and biological processes. Scientists long ago succeeded in achieving the anabiosis of fish and bats; cold does not kill, but preserves them. Moderate cold, of course. Then there is another state—clinical death. The point is, when the heart stops or breathing ceases, an animal or human being does not die immediately. Not at all. The last war gave doctors the opportunity to make a serious study of clinical death. It was found possible for some gravely wounded men to be brought to life again even when the heart had already stopped beating for several minutes; and these were mortally wounded men, mind you! You're a physicist and perhaps you don't know. . . ."

"I have heard something about it," said Niemayer, with a nod.

"The word 'death' loses some of its terror when the medical label 'clinical' is attached to it, doesn't it? Actually there are several intermediate states between life and death: sleep, lethargy and anabiosis, when the human organism is slowed down as compared with its waking state. I've been working on this during the last few years. To slow down the working of the organism to the maximum, anabiosis has to be taken to its limit—to the state of clinical death. I succeeded in doing this. Frogs, rabbits and guinea-pigs were the first to pay for it with their lives. Later, when the rules and regimen of freezing had become quite clear, I risked making my chimpanzee Mimi 'dead' for a spell."

"Ah, yes, I've seen her," exclaimed Niemayer. "A jolly little creature, jumping from chair to chair, begging for sugar-lumps."

"That's right," continued Bern, gravely. "But for four months I had Mimi lying in a little coffin, surrounded by control instruments and chilled almost to freezing-point."

With nervous fingers Bern selected another cigarette.

"Finally came the most important and essential experiment," he continued. "I experimented on myself, underwent full anabiosis. It was last year. You probably remember the word going round that Professor Bern was gravely ill. Actually it was more than that, I was 'dead' for the whole of six months. And I can tell you, Niemayer, it's a most peculiar sensation, if one can speak in such a way about complete absence of any sensations. In ordinary sleep we do perceive, if only belatedly, the rhythm of time—but this wasn't so, not then. It was something like the unconsciousness of narcosis, then complete silence and darkness. Then the return to life. By the way, there was nothing on the other side. . . ."

Bern was sitting at ease, his legs sprawled out, his lean, suntanned arms clasping the back of his head. Behind the spectacle lenses his eyes were pensive.

"The Sun . . . a sphere of light feebly lighting one corner of infinite, black space. All round it other spheres, smaller and cold. All the life on them depends on the Sun alone. . . . And then, mankind—tribes of thinking animals—appeared on one of these spheres. How did mankind originate? There are countless legends and hypotheses about it.

"One thing, though, is certain: the birth of mankind required some tremendous cataclysm—the geological upheaval on our planet that changed the conditions of life of the highest animals, the apes. The consensus of opinion is that this cataclysm was glaciation. The rapid cooling of the northern hemisphere, the scarcity of plant food forced the higher apes to take stones and clubs into their hands in order to get meat, forced them to adapt themselves to working and to love fire."

"That's all very likely," agreed Niemayer.

"And why were there glaciers? Why is it that once upon a time this desert, and even the Sahara, were not deserts at all and plant and animal life developed in them? There is only one logical hypothesis—it connects the ice age with the precession of the Earth's axis. As with every imperfect spinning-top, the Earth's spinning axis precesses—describes slow revolutions, very slow ones: one revolution in twenty-six thousand years. Have a look at this," urged the professor, and with a match he drew an ellipse in the sand, then a little sun at its focus and a small sphere with an inclined axis—the Earth. "As you know, the Earth's axis is inclined to the axis of the ecliptic at an angle of 23°27′. And the Earth's axis describes a cone in space that has a central angle, like this.... You'll forgive me I know for telling you what has been known for ages, but it's important to me, Niemayer. It isn't really a question of an axis, which the Earth hasn't got, anyway. What is important is that in the course of a thousand years changes occur in the position of the Earth relative to the Sun!

"Now, forty thousand years ago, the southern hemisphere was turned towards the Sun and the ice was on the move here in the north. In various places—most probably in Central Asia—tribes of man-apes appeared, herded together by stern geophysical necessity. During this cycle of the precession the first cultures arose. Thirteen thousand years later the northern and southern hemispheres changed places in relation to the Sun, and tribes appeared also in the southern hemisphere.

"The next ice age in the northern hemisphere will begin after twelve or thirteen thousand years. The human race is now incomparably more powerful and capable of coping with this danger ... if mankind still continues to exist at all. But I feel sure that it will be non-existent. With ever increasing speed, made possible by modern science, we are approaching our own end.... I have lived through two world wars: the first as a soldier, the second—in Maidanek. I have been present at atomic and hydrogen bomb tests, and all the same I cannot imagine what a third world war will be like. It is horrible to contemplate! But still worse are the people who, with scientific precision, declare that war will begin in so many months' time. Massed atomic blows against the enemy's industrial centres. Vast radioactive deserts. That's the way some scientists are talking! What's more, they're calculating how to ensure the most effective poisoning of the soil, water and air by radiation. I read an American scientific book recently in which it was proved that an atomic bomb should penetrate not less than 50 feet into the ground in order to throw up the maximum amount of radioactive earth. It's a scientific nightmare!"

Bern leapt to his feet, his hands clutching his head.

The sun had already set and the hot night had begun. A few still, dim stars hung in the dark-blue, swiftly blackening space. The desert, too, was black; only the stars distinguished the sky from the desert.

The professor calmed down and continued talking in a thoughtful, almost expressionless tone of voice. In spite of the heat Niemayer shivered at what the professor was saying in almost a monotone.

"Nuclear bombs will probably not reduce the entire planet to ashes. That won't be essential; but they will saturate the Earth's atmosphere with excessive radioactivity. And you know the effect of radiation on childbirth. For several generations what remains of the human race will give birth to degenerates quite incapable of coping with the new, incredibly complicated conditions of life. Perhaps people will succeed in inventing still more perfect and more powerful weapons of mass suicide. The later the third world war begins, the more terrible it will be. Never yet in my life have I seen men avoiding a chance to fight. And so by the end of the next cycle there will not be a single rational creature left on our cosmic sphere.

"The planet will revolve beneath the Sun for ages and it will be as empty and still as it is in this desert," the professor went on, extending his arms towards the barren sands. "Iron will be destroyed by corrosion, buildings will crumble. Then a new ice-age will appear, thick layers of ice will expunge the dead remains of our unfortunate civilization from the face of the planet. And that will be the end! The earth will be cleansed and ready for a new human race. Today we human beings hold back the development of all animals: we hound them and kill them, we destroy rare breeds. When the human race has disappeared, the liberated animal world will begin a period of vigorous development in numbers and quality. By the time of the new ice-age the higher apes will be sufficiently developed to begin thinking. And so a new race of mankind will arise—let's hope it will be more fortunate than our own."

"But just a minute, Professor!" exclaimed Niemayer. "We're not all suicidal lunatics, after all!"

"You're right there," agreed Bern with a wry smile. "But a single madman can do so much harm that even a thousand sane men will be unable to save the situation. I've decided to be present at the advent of the new human race. The time relay in my apparatus has a radioactive isotope of carbon with a half-period of about eight thousand years." Bern nodded in the direction of the shaft. "The relay is set to wear out in one hundred and eighty centuries; by that time the radiation of the isotope will have become so reduced that the plates of the electroscope will separate and complete the circuit. By then this dead desert will once again have become flowering subtropics, and the most favourable living conditions for the new anthropoids will be just here."

Niemayer jumped to his feet.

"All right, the warmongers are madmen. But what about you and your project?" he said excitedly. "You want to freeze yourself for eighteen thousand years!"

"But why simply 'freeze'?" Bern coolly objected. "Here we have a whole complex of reversible death: cooling down, lulling to sleep, antibiotics...."

"But it's suicide, pure and simple!" shouted Niemayer. "Never will you convince me! Come, it's still not too late."

"No. There's no more risk than with any other complicated experiment. You know yourself that 40 years ago a mammoth carcase was extracted from the eternal ice layer of the Siberian tundra. The flesh was so well preserved that dogs enjoyed eating it. If a mammoth carcase in accidental, natural conditions, could remain fresh for tens of thousands of years, then why can I not preserve myself in scientifically calculated, tested conditions! And your semi-conducting thermoelements of the latest type make it possible, reliably and simply, to transform heat into electric current and at the same time to produce cooling. I take it they won't let me down over a period of eighteen thousand years, will they?"

Niemayer shrugged his shoulders.

"Of course the thermoelements won't let you down. They're perfectly simple structures and the conditions in the shaft are the best they could have; very little fluctuation of temperature, no moisture. . . . They can be guaranteed to last over the period as well as the mammoth did. But what about the rest of the instruments? If a single one of them breaks down during the eighteen thousand years. . . ."

Bern straightened up and stretched himself against the starry background.

"The other instruments won't have to last such a long time. They only have to operate twice: tomorrow morning and again after a period of one hundred and eighty centuries, at the beginning of the next life cycle on our planet. All the rest of the time they will be preserved with me in the cell."

"Tell me honestly, Professor, do you really still believe in the end of our human race?"

"It's a terrible thing to believe," said Bern, pensively. "But I'm a man as well as a scientist. And I want to see for myself. Come on now, let's turn in. We've lots of work ahead of us tomorrow."

In spite of being very tired, Niemayer slept badly. It may have been due to the heat or the impression made by what the professor had said, but his brain was over-excited and sleep would not come. When the first rays of the sun touched the tents he was glad to get up. Bern, lying near by, immediately opened his eyes.

"Shall we make a start?"

A scrap of extraordinarily blue sky was visible from the cool depths at the bottom of the shaft. Underground the narrow shaft widened out. In a niche stood the installation which Niemayer and Bern had been setting up during the past few days. The strong cables of the thermoelements ran to it from the sandy walls of the shaft.

For the last time Bern tested the working of all the instruments in the cell. At his instructions, Niemayer cut out a small hollow at the top of the shaft, inserted a charge in it and ran wiring to the cell. The preparations finished, they scrambled out to the surface. The professor lit a cigarette and looked round him.

"The desert looks wonderful today, doesn't it? Well, my dear colleague, that appears to be all. In a few hours' time I shall cut off my own life; it's what you so banally refer to as suicide. Take a simpler view of things. Life is an enigma, people are constantly trying to see the sense of it; just a short stroke on the endless ribbon of time. Just let life consist of two 'strokes'.... Come now, say a parting word to me, we've hardly ever had a chance to talk about trifles."

Niemayer bit his lip and for a moment said nothing.

"I simply don't know what to say! I still can't believe you'll really go through with it. I'm afraid to believe you will."

"Hm! You've calmed me down a bit," said Bern, smiling. "When there's someone else to worry about you, it's not so terrible. We won't sadden each other by prolonging the sepa-

194

ration. When you get back, just stage the accident with the helicopter, as we agreed. You know without my telling you that secrecy is the essential condition of this experiment. In two weeks' time the autumn sand-storms will begin. Good-bye. And don't look at me like that: I'll outlive you all!"

The professor shook hands with Niemayer.

"I suppose the cell will only take one person," said Niemayer, jerkily.

"Yes, only one." There was an expression of warm sympathy on Bern's face as he continued: "I think I'm beginning to regret I didn't try to persuade you earlier." Then, one foot on the step, he added: "In five minutes' time get yourself clear of the shaft!" His hoary head disappeared down it.

Bern bolted the cell door behind him, exchanged his clothing for a sort of diving-suit with numerous tubes attached and laid himself down on the floor on a plastic mattress moulded into shape to fit the contours of his body. He shifted his body a little; nothing was pressing on any part of him. The signal lamps on the control panel opposite indicated that the instruments were ready.

He felt for the button of the detonating fuse, hesitated for a second, then pressed it. There was a slight tremor, but no sound penetrated the cell. The shaft was now covered over. With a final movement Bern switched on the pumps of the cooling apparatus and the narcotic feeder, dropped his arm into the appropriate hollow of the mattress, fixed his gaze on a small, shining sphere in the ceiling and began steadily to count the seconds. . . .

At the surface, Niemayer heard a muffled explosion and watched a column of sand and dust fly up into the air. Bern's cell was now buried under a layer of 45 feet of earth. Niemayer looked round him; it felt eerie in the suddenly silent desert. Then he walked slowly to the helicopter.

Some five days after he had conscientiously blown up the helicopter, he reached a small Mongolian settlement.

Just one week later the autumn winds began to drive the sand-hills from one part of the desert to the other, removing all traces of the hollow. The sands, countless as time itself, smoothed out the last camp of Bern's small expedition; nothing remained to distinguish the spot from its surroundings.

———

A flickering, diffused green light appeared slowly out of the darkness. When it became steady, Professor Bern realized that this was the signal lamp of the radioactive relay. So it had worked!

His conscious mind gradually cleared. To the left he saw the fallen plates of the electroscope of the perpetual clock—it marked between "19" and "20." "The middle of the twentieth millennium," his brain was working accurately and he was filled with a sensation of restrained agitation.

"Now to test the body." Cautiously he moved arms, legs and neck; he opened and shut his mouth. The body was responding, except for the right leg, which was still numb. It had evidently "gone to sleep," or else the temperature had risen too rapidly. He made a few more energetic movements to warm himself up; then he stood up. He took a look at the instruments and found the hands of the voltmeters had dropped. Evidently, the accumulators had run down a little during the defrosting. Bern switched on all the thermal batteries and the hands immediately quivered and moved upwards. At once his thoughts turned to Niemayer: the thermoelements had not let him down. The memory evoked a strange, painful duality of thought: "But it's ages since Niemayer existed; nobody exists any more. . . ."

His glance turned to the metal sphere in the ceiling; it was dark, not shining at all. Bern began to get impatient. Again he looked at the voltmeters: the accumulators were not charging very well, but if the thermo-batteries were switched on as well there should be sufficient power for the ascent to the surface. He changed his clothing and went up through the trapdoor in the ceiling of the chamber to the cover with its automatic screwhead.

He pulled down the switch and the electric motors hummed as they began to revolve. The screw of the cover had begun to bore into the soil. The floor of the chamber shifted slightly. With a sense of relief Bern perceived that the cover was slowly moving upwards. . . .

Finally the dry crunching of stones against metal came to an end; the cover had reached the surface. Bern tried to unscrew the nuts on the door with a special key, but it was not easy and he scratched his fingers. The bluish light of dusk showed through a crack. A few more efforts and the professor emerged from the cover.

The dark, silent forest lay all round in the fresh evening dusk. The cone of the cover had bored through the soil near the roots of a tree; its mighty trunk carried a thick crown of leaves high into the darkening sky. Bern was horrified at the thought of what he had escaped: supposing the tree had been growing just half a yard to the left! He went up to the tree and felt it; the porous bark was damp to the touch. What kind of tree was it? He would have to wait until morning to find out.

Professor Bern returned to the cover and checked his supplies: tins of food and water, compass, revolver. He lit a cigarette. "So far my idea was correct," was the thought uppermost in his mind. "The desert is covered with forest. I must see whether the radioactive clocks have kept good time, but how?"

The trees were not very close together and between them the stars shining in the sky were clearly visible. Bern looked up and an idea flashed through his mind: Vega should now be the "polar star."

He picked up his compass and set off in the darkness to find a tree with low branches. Clumsily he began to climb it. The branches scraped against his face and their rustling scared a bird which flew off the branch with a loud squawk, striking Bern a painful blow on the cheek. Its strange cry resounded in the forest for some time. Panting for breath, the professor seated himself on an upper branch and looked up into the sky.

By now it was quite dark. Above him spread the totally unfamiliar sky with its abundance of bright stars. His eyes searched for the familiar constellations: where was the Great Bear and Cassiopea? Not there, and, indeed, how could they be? After thousands of years the stars had moved and thrown all the old charts of the stars into confusion. But the Milky Way still spanned the sky in a misty strip of star-dust. Professor Bern brought the compass close to his eyes and watched the feebly luminous needle pointing to the north. He turned his gaze northwards. Low above the black horizon where the starry sky ended, Vega, the brightest star in the sky, shed its greenish, almost still light! Near by smaller stars shone out, the distorted constellation of Lyra.

All doubts were now dispelled. Bern was indeed at the beginning of the new cycle of the precession—in the twentieth millennium.

He spent the night in reflection. He could not sleep and was impatient for the dawn. At last the stars grew dim and finally disappeared, and a grey, transparent mist rose among the trees. Bern looked at the thick, tall grass at his feet and discovered it was a most gigantic moss! Just as he had expected, fern-like vegetation, the most primitive, the hardiest, had begun to develop after the glacial period.

With heightened interest Bern strode through the forest. His feet became entangled in the long, pliant stalks of the moss, the heavy dew quickly soaked his shoes. Obviously the season was already autumn. The leaves on the trees were a riot of green, red, yellow and orange. The trees themselves and their coppery-red bark attracted his attention. The leaves stood out against the other fresh, darkish-green colouring. He went closer. They resembled pines, yet instead of pine needles, they had rough leaves, sharply-pointed like sedges and smelling of resin.

Gradually the forest began to come to life. A light rustling breeze dispersed the last of the mist. The sun rose high above the trees; it was the old familiar sun, grown no older in its blinding brilliance. It had not changed in the slightest in one hundred and eighty centuries.

Professor Bern walked on, stumbling over the roots of trees, pushing back his spectacles which slipped from his nose every time he was jolted. Suddenly there was a crackle of twigs and gruntig sounds. Out of the trees appeared the brown trunk of some beast with a cone-shaped head. "A wild boar," Bern decided. But it was not like they used to be. It had a horn over its snout. Catching sight of Bern, the boar stood stock-still for a second, then made off among the trees, whining. "Aha! Scared of man," thought the professor, watching it in astonishment. But suddenly his heart missed a beat: there were dark, damp marks on the bedewed, grey moss, which distinctly crossed the clearing. They were the prints of bare human feet.

Professor Bern bent down over one footprint. It was flat and the large toe was well separated from the others. Could he really have foreseen so accurately? Was it a human being that had passed here recently? He forgot everything else and began to follow the footprints, bending down to see more clearly. "So there are human beings here and judging by the fact that wild boars are afraid of them, they must be strong and agile."

The encounter came about unexpectedly. The prints led to a clearing from which Bern first of all heard sharp, guttural exclamations and then spied several creatures covered with greyish-yellow fur. Their figures were bent and they were standing by some trees, holding on to the branches with their arms. They looked in the direction of the approaching professor. Bern stopped walking, threw caution to the winds and stood staring at the bipeds. They were, without doubt, anthropoid apes: hands with five fingers, low foreheads sloping back from prominent bumps over the brows, which protruded above the tiny nose and the jaw. He noticed that two of them had some sort of skin cloak slung over their shoulders.

So it had really happened! Bern suddenly experienced a feeling of angry, nostalgic isolation. "Here we are, full cycle· what existed tens of thousands of years ago has returned after thousands of years of the future. . . ."

Meanwhile one of the anthropoid apes moved towards Bern and gave a shout; the cry sounded imperative. Professor Bern noticed that he carried a heavy tree club in his hand. He was evidently the leader; the others moved forward behind him. Only then did he realize the danger. The apes came closer, hobbling clumsily but quite rapidly on their half-bent legs. The professor fired all the cartridges from his revolver into the air and fled into the forest.

That was his mistake. Had he run out into the open, the apes would most likely not have overtaken him, as their feet were still poorly adapted to upright walking. But in the forest they had the advantage. They swung from the branches of one tree to the next with sharp, triumphant cries. Some of them took huge, swinging leaps. In front of them all was the "leader" with his club.

Behind him the professor heard exultant, savage shouts as the man-apes overtook him. For some reason the thought flashed through his mind that it was something like a lynching. He should not have run away; the fleer is always defeated. His heart beat fast, the sweat streamed down his face, his legs seemed to be stuffed with cotton wool. Suddenly his terror vanished, expelled by a lucid, relentless thought: "Why run away? What is there to escape from? This is the end of the experiment." He stopped running, twined his arms round a tree trunk and turned to face his pursuers.

The "leader" was in the front of the chase. He was brandishing the club over his head. Professor Bern saw his small, firece yet cowardly eyes with the reddish, hairy lids, the bared teeth. The hair on the right shoulder was scorched. "So they know what fire is," Bern hurriedly noted. The "leader" rushed up et out a yell and brought down the club on the professor's head. The terrible blow felled the scientist to the ground, his face covered with blood. For a moment he lost consciousness, then came to in time to see other apes rushing at him, the leader raising its arm again for the final blow, and something silvery shining against the blue sky.

"Yet all the same mankind is developing anew," was his thought just one second before the club came down on his head and deprived him of the ability to think any more.

A few days later the following statement was published in the Bulletin of the World Academy:

"On September 12, 18,879 of the Era of Liberated Man, the mutilated body of a man was discovered in an Asiatic reserve on the territory of the former Gobi desert. The man was taken unconscious by emergency iono-plane to the nearest Life Restoring Unit. He has not yet recovered consciousness, but his life is now out of danger.

"The structure of the skull and nervous system and what remains of the man's clothing indicate that he belonged to the beginning of our Era. How a man of that period, in view of the low level of scientific and technical development at that time, was able to keep himself alive for more than eighteen millennia is at present unclear. A special expedition of the Academy is conducting energetic investigations in the reserve.

"We know that for several generations biologists have been carrying out experimental work in the Gobi reserve to test the correctness of the hypothesis concerning the origin of man and the human race. Their efforts have been successful in producing a species of man-apes which as regards the level of development are an intermediary link between the anthropoid apes and the pithecanthropes which existed hundreds of thousands of years ago. A tribe of these man-apes inhabited the area close to the place where the Man of the Past was found. It seems likely that it was their encountering him that ended so tragically for him.

"The palaeontological section of the Academy proposes that a closer watch should be kept on the reserve in the future. Special attention should be paid to ensuring that the man-apes do not use their working tools as weapons of slaughter, since were they to do so, it would have a harmful effect on the development of their intellect.

"Presidium of the World Academy."